So Molly Matthews had a little girl

Three years old maybe? Molly had done exactly as he'd predicted she would. She hadn't learned a thing from her infatuation with him. Hurt by what she'd seen as Luke's rejection, she'd simply turned to another man to soothe her wounded pride. And now she had a child.

Luke felt no satisfaction at being proved correct. He'd done what he'd known was right. If, instead, he'd taken advantage of what she'd so trustingly offered him, all those years ago…

That little girl might have been his.

From boardroom...to bride and groom!

Dear Reader,

Welcome to the latest book in our **Marrying the Boss** miniseries, which is also a special story for Mother's Day. We hope you're enjoying our series of tantalizing stories about love in the workplace, from some of your favorite Harlequin Romance® authors.

Falling for the boss can mean trouble, so our gorgeous heroes and lively heroines all struggle to resist their feelings of attraction for each other. But somehow love always ends up top of the agenda. And it isn't just a nine-to-five affair.... Mixing business with pleasure carries on after hours—and ends in marriage!

Happy reading!

The Editors

The Boss and the Baby
Leigh Michaels

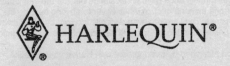

TORONTO • NEW YORK • LONDON
AMSTERDAM • PARIS • SYDNEY • HAMBURG
STOCKHOLM • ATHENS • TOKYO • MILAN • MADRID
PRAGUE • WARSAW • BUDAPEST • AUCKLAND

ISBN 0-373-03552-7

THE BOSS AND THE BABY

First North American Publication 1999.

Copyright © 1999 by Leigh Michaels.

This edition published by arrangement with Harlequin Books S.A.

® and TM are trademarks of the publisher. Trademarks indicated with ® are registered in the United States Patent and Trademark Office, the Canadian Trade Marks Office and in other countries.

Printed In U.S.A.

CHAPTER ONE

MOLLY MATTHEWS straightened the lapels of her jacket and took a deep breath as she looked herself over in the guest room mirror. Her suit was stylishly cut, but the neutral beige wool didn't scream for attention. The pale yellow blouse was softly feminine, but it was neither lacy nor revealing. Her jewelry was limited to tiny gold earrings and the slightly splashier pin nestled in the geometric pattern of the scarf tucked casually around her throat. Her hair was swept back and up into a neat twist, revealing a slim, straight neck...

And a bruise on the left side of her jawline, halfway between chin and ear.

Molly sighed. She'd done the best she could to camouflage the yellowing stain with makeup, and she'd just have to hope that the casual observer would think the shadow on her jaw was no more than a reflection of the darkest color in the brilliant scarf.

She gave a final pat to the folds of the scarf and turned away from the mirror. As job applicants went, she was as well turned out as it was possible to be—tasteful instead of high-fashion, with nothing about her clothes or manner that could create a bad first impression with an interviewer. "Unless he's put off by someone who looks so seriously vanilla," she told herself, and tried to laugh. But this appointment was too important to make into a joke. The job she was seeking...

Though, to be technical, she wasn't interviewing for a job at all, she was vying for a contract. And she wasn't an applicant, exactly. She was a business proprietor contacting a prospective client who had indicated an interest in her skills.

If Warren Hudson liked her ideas and was impressed enough with her abilities to give her this assignment, she'd have a few months of work ahead of her. Enough, perhaps—if she was careful—to build a foundation under her new small business.

Matthews and Associates was, at the moment, very new and very small. Molly could see the whole of it, in fact, from where she stood. The bed in her parents' guest room had been pushed aside to leave room for a folding table, which held a telephone so newly installed that Molly hadn't yet memorized the number and a computer with the sales stickers still attached. Under the table was a box of office supplies in untouched wrappings and a bag containing business cards on which the ink was barely dry.

She had bought carefully and frugally, but that corner of the room represented a good chunk of her worldly resources. Which was why it was so important for Molly Matthews and her fictional associates to impress Warren Hudson this afternoon.

That was the truly frightening part, Molly thought—being so very clearly on her own. Always before, even during a few weeks when she'd been between jobs, she'd had a safety net of sorts. But this time, instead of using her last paycheck as a cushion while she sought another corporate position, she'd invested it in her future. And—of course—Bailey's future, too.

Remember Bailey, she told herself. *You'd take a bigger risk than this for her sake.*

Molly picked up the dark brown calfskin portfolio that contained the best examples of her work, tucked it under her arm and closed the guest room door behind her.

From the kitchen, Bailey called, "Mommy! Come and see!"

Molly paused in the arched doorway between kitchen

and hall. For a moment her eyes rested on her daughter, kneeling on a kitchen chair so she was tall enough to work on the tabletop, industriously wielding a blue crayon. Bailey's dark brown hair, a couple of shades deeper than her mother's, was combed into twin ponytails today, each adorned with a big pink bow that matched her corduroy overalls.

Bailey looked at her mother and grinned, and Molly's heart turned over. *Yes,* she thought. *I'd take a much bigger risk than this—for Bailey.*

"What a pretty picture, darling," she said.

From across the table came a light, almost brittle laugh. "Since no one could possibly guess what it's supposed to be, I'd say that's a safe comment."

Molly moved the crayon into a position where Bailey had better control and looked levelly at her sister. "Hello, Megan. It's good to see you."

Her sister, she noted, had pushed her chair well back from the table. Molly wasn't surprised that Megan Matthews Bannister would maintain a safe distance between her creamy white cashmere sweater and Bailey's crayon. If Bailey had chosen paints this afternoon, Megan would probably have retreated all the way to the deck, despite the crisp breeze coming off Lake Superior.

Megan tossed her head. The golden highlights in her light brown hair almost shimmered with the movement. Though it was only April, the streaks in her hair and the tone of her skin made it seem as if she'd spent weeks in the sun.

But of course she had, Molly remembered. Their mother had written, in her dutiful once-a-month letter, about Megan's winter vacation in the Caribbean.

"I dropped by to ask Mom some last-minute questions about the anniversary party," Megan said. "I've been gone so much that everything's been on hold, but the details have to be wrapped up this week."

Of course you wouldn't be coming to visit me, Molly

thought. *Even if we haven't seen each other in years. Even if you've never met your niece before. Even if we've been home only a few days...*

She was startled at the bitterness she felt—though the reaction was really nothing new. Even in their teenage years, Megan—popular, beautiful and graceful—had never had much time to spare for a younger sister who had still been gangly and awkward, an unwelcome tagalong. And now that they were adults...

Megan's still the socialite, Molly reflected, almost wryly. Megan had married a wealthy man from a good family. She belonged to all the best clubs, went to all the best parties, worked for all the best charities, vacationed in all the best spots, knew all the best people.

While I... Molly's gaze rested thoughtfully on the top of Bailey's head. The part that separated the child's ponytails was crooked, and one of her bows had slipped, but when Molly tried to straighten it, Bailey squirmed away, more interested in her drawing than her appearance.

Molly gave up and looked around the kitchen. "Where is Mother, by the way? She said she'd watch Bailey this afternoon while I go to my appointment."

Bailey's lower lip crept out, and her chin trembled. "Don't want Gramma," she said. "I want you to stay, Mommy."

Molly's heart twisted. *Of course she doesn't want Gramma. The child hardly knows her. It's only been four days—*

She leaned over Bailey and dropped a kiss on her hair. "I know, darling, and I'd stay here with you if I could. But remember we talked about my new job? I have to go see a man—"

Megan drew a breath that sounded like a sharp hiss. "What happened to your face? You look as if you've been in a brawl."

Molly's hand went automatically to the dark spot on her jaw. "Oh, this. It's nothing, really."

Her mother spoke from the doorway. "*Nothing?* She says Bailey kicked her." Alix Matthews's dark tone implied that she had her doubts about the explanation.

"Kicked—" Megan's tone was speculative.

Alix nodded and walked briskly across the kitchen. "In my day a child who did that—if, of course, she really did…"

"I told you it was a somersault that went wrong, Mother. Bailey didn't mean to hurt me, it was an accident."

Bailey frowned. She held up her drawing to look at it and then put her blue crayon down and selected a green one.

Megan didn't look convinced.

Alix's gaze skimmed over Molly. "That suit's all right, I suppose. At least it fits. You're not going to wear a ring?"

Molly wanted to groan. Instead, she said dryly, "Remember, Mother? I'm divorced."

"I still think that a discreet little gold band…"

Molly didn't want to listen to any more. "I don't expect to be gone for more than a couple of hours, Mom. Thanks for taking care of Bailey."

Alix didn't answer, but she looked at her watch.

Molly leaned over the little girl, and the scent of baby shampoo tickled her nose. Bailey was almost four, but she was small for her age, and her wiry little body still fit perfectly in her mother's arms. "I'll come back just as soon as I can, Bailey," she said. "You be good for Grandma, all right? And maybe tonight we'll go get ice cream."

Bailey's eyes lit. "Pink ice cream?"

"Bribing a child," Alix said, "is never a good idea."

Molly bit her tongue. The tip of it was beginning to feel sore after four days of Alix's advice, but she absolutely would not argue with her mother about how to raise her child as long as she was living under the woman's roof. And if Molly pointed out the fact that she'd been doing quite well on her own, Alix would probably just sniff and say that opinions differed—so why bother to say it?

One more reason, Molly told herself, *that I have to do well in this presentation.* If Warren Hudson liked her work enough to give her a contract to produce his company's publications, then before long she and Bailey could move to a place of their own.

And that day couldn't come fast enough for Molly.

Her father had warned her that Warren Hudson's business had changed a great deal in the years since she'd left Duluth. Still, Molly wasn't fully prepared for Meditronics' complex of sleek new buildings, nestled close together and tucked almost into the side of the steep and rugged hill that pressed the city close to Lake Superior. And she certainly wasn't prepared for the security post at the main entrance.

There had always been a gate house, of course. In the days when her father had been a line worker in Meditronics' factory, building medical machinery, there had been around-the-clock guards who checked each employee and visitor in and out. Now, in a well-sheltered niche at the side of the main drive was what looked like a parking-lot ticket machine with a keyboard attached. Molly lowered her car window and eyed the machine, which beeped, clicked and said, in a pleasant—though mechanical—masculine voice, "Please enter your name, last name first."

Molly obediently tapped the keys. The machine digested the information and said, "Please enter the name of the person you wish to visit, last name first."

"I liked the old days better," she murmured as she started to type. "All the guards knew me, and there was never any fuss about getting inside where it was warm to wait for the end of Dad's shift.''

The machine ignored her protest and with an asthmatic whir thrust a card down a chute in its front, announcing, ''While you are inside the plant, please wear this identification badge at all times. You will find Mr. Warren Hudson in the administration building, to your left at the first intersection.''

Molly picked up the card. Its laminated surface was still warm. Under the plastic coating was her name, along with Warren Hudson's, an elaborate bar code and a small photograph of her with her mouth open and her eyes half shut, obviously taken just moments before.

''That's what you get for talking back to the machine,'' she muttered. ''It exacted revenge.'' She fastened the card to her jacket lapel with a clip, which the machine had thoughtfully dispensed, and let her car creep up the main drive to the parking lot outside the administration building.

It isn't too late to back out, said a little voice in the far corner of her brain.

She shook her head almost in surprise. Of course it was too late to cancel this appointment, and she wouldn't back out even if she could. She needed this job, this client.

There are other clients, the voice murmured. *You don't have to go in there and face Warren Hudson.*

That was crazy. There was no reason not to go, she told herself. The only thing Warren Hudson knew about her was that Bernie Matthews was her father.

Are you sure about that?

''Of course that's all he knows,'' she said to herself. ''He'd hardly be interested in the fact that you used to have a terrific crush on his son.'' Molly rubbed her temples and dragged her portfolio from the back seat. She was only suffering from last-minute butterflies. There was always this breathless sensation right before a presentation, when it was too late to do another thing to make the package better.

She was five minutes early when she walked into the executive office suite, and Warren Hudson, his secretary said, was waiting for her. Molly wondered uneasily if that was a good sign or a bad one. Was he simply eager to talk to her because he was excited about this project? Or...

There wasn't time to speculate. The secretary tapped on the half-open walnut door and said, "Ms. Matthews, sir." She stood aside to let Molly pass and added, "Shall I bring the coffee tray in now?"

Molly's gaze went straight to the massive desk set at right angles to the window, which framed a view of the aerial lift bridge and the lake beyond. The water looked gray today, under a halfhearted April sun, and mist hid the far side of the lake.

But Warren Hudson wasn't at his desk. He was seated in a wing chair in a little conversation area nearby, with the *Wall Street Journal* open on his knee. He stood up, folded the newspaper and laid it aside and held out a hand to Molly. "Your father tells me you're just what I'm looking for. Come in, my dear, and let's talk."

He was as big and gruff as Molly remembered, though his hair was entirely silver now, his shoulders stooped a bit, and there was a tremor in his outstretched hand. He waved her to the chair that matched his, and Molly set her portfolio on the deep gray carpet at her feet.

Warren Hudson settled into his chair once more. "So you're back in Duluth. You know, all the time I hear people saying they can't wait to leave this town. The funny thing is how many of them end up coming back here. You've been in Chicago the last few years, right?"

She'd started to wonder when—or if—he was going to let her get a word in. "Most of the time. I worked for a couple of corporations in their publications divisions, doing product brochures and catalogs and annual reports.''

"But with downsizing—" he prompted.

Molly nodded. She wasn't surprised he knew how she'd lost her job. Her father would have told him, just to make it clear that she hadn't been fired for incompetence. "The company decided to eliminate the division and farm out the work to independents.''

"So you elected to start your own business.''

"I'd been thinking about it for a while, and this seemed the right time to give it a try.''

The secretary came in with a delicate china coffee service, and Warren waved a hand toward Molly. The secretary set the tray on the low table in front of her and disappeared once more into her office. Molly noticed that she left the door half-open, and told herself not to fret about it. This conversation was hardly top secret.

Warren said, "Would you pour? I'd appreciate it. I'm a clumsy old soul since I had a stroke a few months back.''

"I'm sorry to hear that. Not a severe one, I hope?'' The scent of the rich, dark brew rose from the china cups as she poured, tugging at Molly's senses.

"Oh, I'm doing all right.'' He put out his left hand for his cup and saucer and sat back, frowning. "I'm still not sure I understand, though. You had contacts in Chicago. People in the business who knew your skills. A possibility of actually doing the same work for the same people, though under a different set of circumstances. Here, you'll have to start from scratch.'' There was a challenge in his voice. "So what really brings you back to Duluth, Molly Matthews?''

It was a question she should have anticipated, and Molly could have kicked herself for not having an answer prepared. To buy a little time, she leaned forward to pour cream into her coffee. "I can still do some of

that work from here, you know. With faxes and overnight delivery services—''

He shrugged. ''Easier yet to do it there. Besides, if
people don't see your face regularly, they tend to forget
you exist.''

''But it's less expensive to start a business here than
in a larger city and to live till it gets off the ground. And
my family offered help in the meantime.'' The image of
Alix looking at her watch as if she was starting a mental
timer flashed into Molly's mind, and she tried to shrug
it off.

He didn't look satisfied, but he didn't press.

''And I have a little girl now,'' she went on. ''I didn't
want to raise her in the city, and this was the best time
to make the move.''

Warren's brow cleared. ''That's right. Your father told
me your marriage didn't work out. I'm sorry.''

Apparently, she thought grimly, *there isn't much my
father didn't tell you.* ''Thank you, sir.'' She kept her
eyes focused on the coffee tray. Would she ever be able
to hear that damned divorce mentioned without feeling
as if she was choking?

It's part of the price of coming home, she reminded
herself.

''When I lost my wife,'' Warren mused. ''Of course,
it was a different sort of ache, but I expect the feeling
of being abandoned is a fairly universal one, don't
you?''

The feeling of being abandoned... Molly could certainly identify with that, but the last thing she wanted
was to be drawn into a discussion about it. ''I'm sure
you understand how painful it is for me to talk about.''

''Of course. There for a minute I forgot you're not
just Bernie Matthews's daughter stopping by for a social
chat.''

Molly forced herself to smile, to play along. ''No, that
would have been Megan.'' She leaned forward to pick

up the coffeepot. "Tell me about the changes at Meditronics since I left."

"How long do you have?" Warren Hudson smiled. "That's why we want to do this project, you know. Next year the company will have been in business for a century. Of course, the products we make have changed a great deal over that time, along with medicine itself. Now we're not only producing medical equipment but support machines. Take our automated gatekeeper, for instance. We designed it to control access to certain areas in hospitals, but it works equally well for other purposes."

"I was going to ask about that." Molly flicked a fingertip against the laminated badge she wore. "What's to prevent someone from typing in any employee's name, getting a badge and wandering freely all over the plant?"

"You don't think the machine's that simpleminded, do you? It doesn't issue a pass till it's made sure the employee's actually here and has authorized a visitor."

"And how does somebody get in if they don't know the name of the person they need to see? Or if they don't have an appointment?"

"Oh, that sets off an entirely different routine. And before you ask what happened to our human security guards, we didn't fire them. A couple of them retired and the rest moved into other jobs. Don't you think the badges are nice?"

"I don't think I'll be ordering reprints of the photo," Molly said wryly.

"That one's certainly not its best work. By the way, the machine keeps those on file, too, so next time you come, it'll compare the two and make sure you're really you."

"In that case, I'll have to remember to reproduce the grimace, or it'll kick me out entirely because I look so different. You were just starting to tell me about the

project you have in mind, Mr. Hudson. My father mentioned that you were looking for someone with
publications experience, but he didn't have many details."

Warren settled deeper into his chair. "We want to use
our hundred years of history to promote Meditronics.
There will be things like updated sales brochures and
new ads, of course, but we have an agency for that. What
you'll be doing is gathering and organizing the history
of the company so the advertising and promotions people can choose the bits that will be most useful."

What you'll be doing. It sounded as if the job was
hers, and some of the tension drained from the muscles
in Molly's neck and shoulders. She cautioned herself,
though, about taking too much for granted. He hadn't
even asked to look at samples of her work.

"But what I'd really like to focus on is a book,"
Warren said. "A nice, glossy hardcover—a complete
history of the company that we could send out to all our
customers."

"A gift as we look forward to serving you for another
century," Molly mused.

"You've got the idea exactly—and it's not a bad slo-
gan. You're sure you're not an advertising specialist?
What do you think, Molly?"

She could see the eagerness in his eyes. He didn't look
his age at all. In fact, he reminded her a little of Bailey
when she'd just come up with a new scheme and was
plotting to win approval so she could try it out.

He was the boss, Molly told herself. All she had to
do was smile and agree, and the job would drop like a
plum into her lap. And it wasn't a bad idea.

Still...

She took a deep breath. "Good, as far as it goes."

The gleam in Warren Hudson's eyes diminished.

"Since books are solid and look valuable," Molly
went on quickly, "most people hesitate to discard

them—so your book will hang around the customer's office and remind him of Meditronics every time he sees it. But I wonder if that's enough. A book may also lie there for years and never be read. If you were to create a video presentation, though—''

Warren shifted in his chair. ''Trying to work yourself out of a job?''

Molly smiled. ''Oh, no. I can do video, too—organize and write and supervise it, at least. And I'm not suggesting you do video instead of the book, but along with it. A video presentation would be more flexible. It could be carried around by your salesmen, used at conventions or sales expositions—and it could also be combined with the book into a slick gift package that nobody could throw away.'' She was on a roll. ''It wouldn't be inexpensive, of course, but...''

''But we're only old once,'' Warren said, and grinned. ''Now that's my kind of attitude, Molly—taking an idea and making it better. In fact, I think there's only one more thing to take care of before we make this deal official—''

He'd want to see examples of her work, of course. Molly reached for the portfolio at her feet.

From the outer office, through the half-open door, floated the sound of a masculine voice, and for a moment she felt as if every joint in her body had locked simultaneously.

But she couldn't be hearing what she thought, she told herself. It was—it had to be—purely a trick of the imagination.

She'd already discovered in the four short days since she'd come home that simply being back in Duluth—driving down London Road, gazing across the lake, walking on the beach—had given new life to old memories. It was only reasonable that sitting in Warren Hudson's office would make her think of his son. She should have expected that. And it was memory, not fact,

that had made her think for an instant that Luke was just
beyond that half-open door. He couldn't be. He was half
a continent away.

The man in the outer office spoke again, and Molly's
heartbeat slowed toward normal. This man's voice was
deeper than Luke's, and richer somehow. The two
weren't really alike at all.

She picked up the calfskin portfolio.

"Oh, good," Warren Hudson said. "I hoped Lucas
would come in time to meet you."

Her fingers went numb, and the portfolio slipped from
her grasp. It tipped flat, and a slim catalog slid halfway
out onto the carpet.

But he's not even in Minnesota anymore, Molly
thought. *He's a fully qualified doctor, and he's in
California.* It had been two years ago at least that her
mother had written that Lucas Hudson had gone to the
West Coast for his internship, and Alix hadn't mentioned
him again after that.

But that didn't mean there'd been no more news about
him, Molly realized, just that Alix hadn't happened to
think of it while she was writing her terse, dutiful, in-
frequent letters.

"Though surely you two knew each other," Warren
said, "before you left Duluth?"

Molly told herself firmly that she had nothing to be
embarrassed about now. She was grown up, and what
had happened years ago didn't matter any more. So what
if she'd had a crush on Lucas Hudson when she was a
kid? So what if the way he'd told her to get over it had
made her want to crawl under the nearest boulder and
die? He'd probably believed he was doing her a favor.

In the long run, she thought, he probably had.

"He was more my sister's age," she said. Luke had
been Megan's friend, not Molly's—that much was true.
The fact that she was also being evasive was beside the
point.

Warren didn't seem to hear, anyway. "Lucas, my boy," he called. "Come in here, if you've got a minute."

The door swung slowly, silently open. *It ought to creak,* Molly thought—although, as far as she was concerned, there was no need for any theatrics to heighten the suspense.

The doorway was large, but it couldn't dwarf the man who stood there with a herringbone tweed jacket slung over one shoulder, his other hand in his trouser pocket. Molly hadn't seen him in years, but she couldn't have missed him even in a crowd. She would never forget how tall he was, though he was broader of shoulder than she remembered. His hair was just as dark, just as thick, and it looked just as soft. He still resembled the athlete he'd been, his body perfectly balanced as if he might leap in any direction in the next moment.

And he was looking at her with casual interest in his hazel eyes. Eyes framed with lashes so long and dark and thick and curly that they were positively indecent.

Looking at her so casually that she wondered if he even remembered the day he'd lectured her about making a fool of herself over him.

Warren said, "Molly and I—you remember Molly Matthews, Lucas? I told you, didn't I, that Bernie was sending her in to see me?"

"You did, Dad." Luke came across the room. "And of course I remember Molly."

His voice *was* both deeper and richer, and Molly could detect nothing but friendliness in his tone. She willed herself not to tremble as she offered her hand, and she succeeded. But even after the brief contact was over, she could feel the warmth of his fingers against her palm.

"Molly," Warren said, "you haven't forgotten my son, Lucas? He's taken over the reins here at Meditronics, after that stroke I was telling you about."

She didn't flinch. She supposed she'd been preparing herself for that statement since she'd heard his voice in the outer office, knowing at some subconscious level that Luke wasn't simply home for a visit.

"In fact," Warren went on, "this whole history project is his idea—I've just agreed to oversee the process. Molly and I have been chatting about it, Lucas, and we've hit it off famously. So with your approval…"

Was Luke's approval the one more thing Warren had been talking of? And if the history project was his idea, did that mean she'd be answering to Luke instead of his father?

It doesn't matter, she told herself. The job hadn't changed in the last ten minutes, only the boss had. But there was something else that hadn't changed—she needed this job just as desperately as ever. If, in order to get it, she had to charm Lucas Hudson…

Then I'll charm him, she told herself grimly. *In fact, I'll be so charming he won't know what hit him.*

CHAPTER TWO

BEFORE MOLLY could embark on her campaign, however—or even decide on a plan of attack—Warren Hudson said, with a note of self-congratulation in his voice, "She's already come up with a much better idea than mine, too. Instead of just doing the book, Molly thinks—"

Hastily, Molly said, "Mr. Hudson, perhaps right now isn't a good time for—"

"Does she, now?" Luke said gently. "Perhaps I should hear all about this exotic idea. And I see you brought samples of your work, Molly? I wouldn't want to bore you, Dad, by making you sit through all this a second time. Why don't I take Molly on into the conference room for a few minutes?"

"It's no prob—" Warren began.

"You look tired, Dad, and I noticed Jason waiting with the car out front when I came in."

Warren pushed himself from his chair. "You might want to practice tossing out hints, Lucas. There's a knack to making them subtle, and you haven't acquired it." He closed the office door very firmly behind him.

Luke chuckled and sat on the arm of the chair Warren had occupied. "Now *that's* a subtle hint. Closing the door, I mean, so that he didn't actually have to say, 'If you want to have Molly all to yourself, all you need to do is ask.'"

She felt a tinge of color steal into her cheeks, and to conceal it she bent to gather the catalog that had spilled out of her portfolio. Of course there was nothing more personal in his comment than a desire to ask a few ques-

21

tions his father might object to. She wondered, for instance, if he guessed that Warren hadn't bothered to check out her work.

Be charming, she reminded herself. The trouble was she had no idea how to begin. In general, of course, being charming was no trouble at all, but this situation was like walking a tightrope. How much charm would be enough? Because if she applied too much, she'd look like...well, like a teenager with a bad crush. And that was an image she'd just as soon not bring into Luke's mind.

"I brought along several different examples of my work," she said. "Brochures, catalogs, an annual report to stockholders. Is there any type you'd like to see first?"

"Not particularly."

Molly frowned. It was odd that he didn't sound interested. "I didn't think to bring a sample of my video work, but I could drop one off—"

Luke shook his head. "No, thanks. I haven't time to sit and watch, and it wouldn't make any difference anyway."

But he'd said he wanted to see... *No,* she corrected herself. He'd implied—no doubt for his father's sake—that he wanted to look over her portfolio. He hadn't actually said anything definite.

And the fact that he didn't seem interested in the caliber of her work didn't necessarily mean he'd already made up his mind not to hire her, either. But Molly's throat grew tight, and she had to work to keep her fear from creeping into her voice. "Then do you want to hear about my idea?"

"The one my father thinks is so brilliant? It's not at the top of my list, no."

Molly stared at him. He seemed perfectly at ease as he sat on the arm of the chair. She couldn't detect so much as a twitch of nervousness, and he was obviously in no hurry to explain himself. His gaze was steady on her face, the hazel eyes narrowed slightly. She wondered for a moment if his eyes ever sparkled with delight any more, or if he always looked a bit suspicious.

She watched as he made up his mind, and she saw determination come into his face—jaw muscles tightening, eyes darkening—and she knew he was bracing himself for something he expected to be unpleasant.

Almost bitterly, she thought that Warren had been a long way off the mark. Luke could be very subtle indeed when he wanted to be—though Molly was having no trouble getting the hint.

She gathered her samples and slid them neatly into the portfolio, zipped it shut and stood up. "I suppose the polite thing to do would be to thank you for the opportunity to prove my fitness for this job, but since you didn't give me that opportunity, Luke, I won't bother."

His eyebrows arched slightly. "Sit down, Molly."

"So, since you're not going to have to waste your time telling me that I won't be working on your father's project, won't you at least take ten seconds to tell me why? Don't you think I've grown up enough to handle the job, is that it?"

"Have you?" His voice was little more than a growl.

"I've certainly shed a number of idiotic illusions!"

"You had plenty of them to shed, as I recall. Now if you'll stop jumping to conclusions and sit down..."

She forced herself to take a slow, deep breath, but she didn't return to her chair. She clasped her portfolio in both hands and looked straight at him. "Well?"

"It's interesting, however," Luke mused, "that you picked up so quickly on the fact that I don't want to give you this job." He strolled to the window.

"Oh, that took great intuition." She couldn't quite keep the sarcasm out of her voice. "Just because you had no interest in my ideas or my qualifications—"

Luke's voice cut across hers. "Because not examining your portfolio or questioning your plans could just as logically mean the exact opposite—that I'd already decided you were hired, so your credentials didn't matter a damn." He turned to face her. "Couldn't it?"

Molly felt as if she were choking. She'd really put her foot in her mouth this time. If there was a way to be more efficient at ruining her chances, she couldn't imagine what it would be.

But she couldn't have been so wrong, she thought frantically. The way Luke had looked at her *wasn't* the way an employer viewed a successful candidate.

"The truth is," Luke said, "I don't want to give anyone this job. But since I have to hire someone, and my father seems to have his mind made up, it might as well be you."

Molly stared at him, aghast. "Well, isn't that just terrific? Your enthusiasm overwhelms me, Luke. I've never before been offered employment under such welcoming circumstances. I'm absolutely honored, but if I didn't need this job—"

Her conscience whispered, *This is how you define 'charming'?* Too late Bailey's face flashed before her, creased in the silly grin her mother loved best, reminding Molly how important this was. No matter how reluctantly, he'd offered her the job. She told herself that was the only thing that should matter now—but she wasn't quite convinced.

"Cut out the sarcasm, Molly. It's nothing personal."

"Oh, now *that* makes me feel much better." Pure puzzlement crept in alongside her frustration. "Though if you actually didn't intend to insult me, I don't quite see why you even wanted a private conversation."

"I certainly didn't intend any insult. I was going to start by telling you the job was yours, but before I could say a word you got up and started to stamp out."

Molly thought about it for a moment and conceded

that he might have a point. Still... "You couldn't have told me the job was mine with your father in the room? If that was all you had to say—"

Luke shook his head. "I wanted to make sure you understand what's really going on here, and I could hardly explain in front of my father that you'll actually be working for me, not for him."

"Now *that* sounds interesting." Her head was spinning, her knees shaking, and she welcomed the excuse to sit down. "So what have you got in mind? And how do you propose to keep him from finding out you've stolen his employee?"

This time Luke settled on the edge of the chair, not the arm. At least, Molly thought, he wasn't looming over her at the moment, but the set of his jaw was threatening nonetheless.

"I'm not stealing anybody. I just have an extra set of job requirements that I don't want my father to know about."

"Oh, this I can't wait to hear," Molly muttered.

Luke leaned forward, elbows on knees and hands clasped. "After my father's stroke," he said, "he lost interest in things. Almost everything, in fact, except the past, which he talked about endlessly and morbidly until it seemed he was retreating into his memories altogether."

Molly frowned. "Then why are you encouraging him to think about the plant's history? He said this project was your idea."

"Oh, it's my idea, all right." Luke sounded almost grim. "You might even call this a last-ditch effort to focus him onto something positive. If he wants to dwell on the past, fine—I give up. But there's a difference between just pondering it over and over and finding ways to use that history to help the company in the future."

"The difference between looking back and looking forward."

There was a gleam in his eyes that might have been appreciation. Or more likely, Molly thought irritably, it was surprise that she'd actually understood.

"And you want me to help manipulate him," she went on.

"So far, it seems to be working. Today is the first time in weeks he's been in the office."

So that's why he was waiting for me with nothing better to do than read the newspaper, Molly thought. "I'm sure his reluctance to hang around Meditronics has nothing to do with your sunny presence and the fact that you've taken over his job since he got sick." She looked around the room. "In fact, is this office his or yours these days?"

"Mine." Luke's voice was stiff.

"No wonder he's been staying home."

"Look, Molly, he may have left you with the impression that I came charging in here two minutes after his stroke, riding my big white horse and determined to take over Meditronics—but the fact is I've been here for well over a year. I was already running things long before he got sick. But that doesn't mean he wasn't still involved. He's chairman of the board. He came to work every day. So when he stopped expressing opinions—or even having them, it seemed—of course I started to get worried."

"So the medical career didn't work out, after all," Molly mused.

"It's not a bad background for selling equipment to hospitals. But about my father—let's get this clear right now, Molly. The only thing that's important about this book idea is that Warren believes in it."

"And you're not really hiring me to help with the book, but to reawaken his interest in life."

"Something like that. You can start tomorrow. We'll find you an office down the hall."

"And if I'm successful," she mused, "just as soon as your father starts being more interested in Meditronics' future than its past, I suppose you'll cut the whole project loose and I'm out of a job, just like that." She shook her head. "You know, it may not have been very wise of you to tell me this, after all."

"Pull that miracle off, and I'll pay you for a book you don't even have to finish. I might even add a nice bonus."

Molly rested her chin on her tented fingertips and considered. "The bonus is a nice touch. Of course, all I have to do is tell your father what you're up to—"

"You said," he reminded, "that you need this job."

He didn't miss a trick, did he? "True enough. Throw in a good recommendation for me to every business you come into contact with, and you're on."

Luke countered, "The most I'll promise is an honest letter of introduction. And as for recommendations, I'll give you one right now—if you're headed for another business appointment, you might want to wipe the smudge off your face."

Before she could stop herself, Molly's hand flew to cover the bruise on her jaw. *Laugh it off,* she ordered herself. *Tell him the somersault story.*

But she couldn't force the words out. Instead, she said lamely, "It's nothing."

His eyes narrowed, and he tipped his head as if to study her more closely.

Molly picked up her portfolio and started toward the outer office. "I'll settle for your promise of a letter of introduction, Luke, but only because it will end up being the same thing as a recommendation, anyway."

"Will it?" He opened the door for her. "I certainly hope you're right."

Luke closed the office door behind Molly and settled into the deep leather chair behind his desk. He'd done

all he could. Now it was simply a matter of waiting to
see whether the treatment would be effective. If anybody
could needle a man out of a state of apathy, he thought
it would be Molly Matthews. He'd seen more liveliness
in his father's eyes today than there'd been in months—
and she'd certainly had Luke in the mood to wring her
dainty little neck. *So the medical career didn't work out
after all....* He was half-surprised she hadn't asked if the
problem was that he fainted at the sight of blood.

But she knew her job now, and he supposed she'd set
about it in her unique way. One thing was certain—there
was no point in giving any more thought to Molly
Matthews in the meantime.

He pulled a stack of correspondence from the in basket, turned on the mini cassette recorder he used for
dictation and leaned back to consider his answers.

But the tape spun uselessly, for his favorite thinking
position, with his elbow propped on the arm of the black
leather chair and his jaw leaning against his hand, reminded him of the discoloration on Molly's face.

It's nothing, she had said. But she'd given herself
away by touching it like that. If it had been only a
smudge, she wouldn't have known where it was.

Somebody had socked her in the jaw.

And it's none of your business who or why, Luke reminded himself. He'd hired her for a purpose, not for
old times' sake. She was no longer the annoying kid
whom he'd rescued now and then from treetops, under-
tows or merciless teasing. She was no longer the coltish
adolescent whose pitifully adoring green eyes had made
him so uncomfortable. She was no longer the naive girl
who had tearfully insisted she would love him forever,
no matter what....

In the last five years, Luke thought, Molly Matthews's
body might have acquired soft curves in all the right
places, but the rest of her had honed down to a knife's
edge. She'd lost her illusions, all right.

A fist in the face will do that to you. Especially if it happens regularly.

Some women, he told himself, were hard to figure out.

Molly would have given anything to be able to drive past her parents' house and head north, up the old scenic highway toward Two Harbors. She longed for the freedom to drive until she'd left all her frustrations behind. Or perhaps she'd pull off the road and walk on the pebbly beach and listen to the lake until the timeless rhythm of the waves washed her tension away.

But she'd been gone much longer than she'd expected, and she didn't dare take extra advantage of her mother. Just because Alix had offered to baby-sit today didn't mean she ever would again.

Another thing for the list tomorrow, Molly thought. Now that she had her first client, she'd have to line up steady day care. And thanks to Luke, she was going to need more of it than she'd expected. She'd hoped to do most of her work at home, where she could keep one eye on Bailey. In fact, with access to the right archives, she could design and produce Warren Hudson's book almost anywhere. But if he wasn't involved on a daily basis, she could hardly spark his interests in once more taking up his real job—and that meant hanging around Meditronics a whole lot more than she'd planned on.

Obviously, by the time this was done she'd be able to put that bonus Luke had mentioned to good use. If she earned it.

But how hard could that be? She'd bet anything Warren Hudson was already starting to come out of his shell. With or without her—or the book, either, for that matter—she suspected he'd be plunging into the mainstream within a few weeks. Even without the bonus, Luke was paying good money for nothing.

And he can afford to, she told herself. *So don't feel*

sorry for him. He offered this deal, you didn't twist his arm.

Besides, he wouldn't be getting *nothing,* anyway. No matter what, he'd end up with something out of the deal—even if it was only a book of company history that he didn't want.

And considering the way he'd looked at her just before he'd offered her the job—like a man with a toothache facing the dentist's drill, knowing it was both unpleasant and unavoidable—Molly thought that was about what he deserved.

Alix was in the kitchen, chopping something that looked suspiciously like chicory. She looked up when Molly came in. "I'm making Chicken Crecy," she said. "I hope Bailey will eat it."

Molly hoped so, too. The dish smelled wonderful to her, but with a three-year-old one never quite knew. "Well, it's making me hungry, so if she doesn't like it she has no taste at all. Is she asleep?"

"No, your father came home and took her up to Knife River to hunt for agates." Alix's tone left no doubt as to her feelings about Bernie's choice of pastime.

"I don't suppose Megan went along." Molly's voice was droll. Megan in a white cashmere sweater, hunting agates on the beach, was the most unlikely picture she could think of.

"Of course not. She and Rand are going to a dinner party tonight."

In the four days Molly had been home, this must be the third party she'd heard about. She wondered when Megan and Rand ever had time to talk to each other. On the drive to the parties, perhaps? "Can I help with anything, Mom?"

"No, it's all done. Did you get the contract?"

Molly nodded. "It's not quite what I expected, though—it's going to be more like a regular job. I'd hoped to be able to bring a lot of the work home, but it looks like I'll be spending more time at Meditronics than I'd bargained for.'' She hung her jacket over the back of a chair and started to rinse the few dishes Alix had left in the sink. "So I'll have to start looking for day care tomorrow."

Alix frowned. "If that's a hint that I should volunteer to keep Bailey every day—"

Molly's hand clenched on the scrubbing brush, and her voice was taut. "Of course it wasn't, Mother. You're doing so much for me already, how could I possibly expect any more?"

A booming voice from the back door said, "Don't be hasty about this, Alix." Bernie Matthews ducked through the doorway with Bailey perched on his shoulders, dipping just far enough so her head cleared the top of the casing.

The child giggled and clutched at his hair. "Do it again, Grampa!"

Bernie obliged. "She's the only granddaughter you've got, Alix. Now that you've got the chance to know her, grab it—or else don't be surprised, when she's old enough to interest you, that she doesn't want to come and visit."

Molly saw the irritation in her mother's eyes and intervened. "She's right, Dad. It's too much to expect her to do. And I'd better start looking, anyway. It'll get even tougher to find day care when the school year ends and everybody's scrambling to get kids settled for the summer."

"I don't want to go to day care." Bailey sounded mutinous.

"You know, Molly, I hadn't thought of it that way," Bernie mused. "Taking care of a child *is* awfully hard work."

Molly opened her mouth to point out that wasn't quite what she'd said.

"Of course you haven't thought of it that way," Alix

snapped. "You take her out on the beach and let someone else clean up the mess!"

Bernie winked at Molly. "And Alix has been starting
to slow down and lose some of the pep she had when
she was young."

Alix's eyes flared. "Bern, if you're implying that I'm
getting old—"

"If you're not, why are we celebrating thirty years of
marriage the end of this month?"

"Because Megan thought we shouldn't let the occa-
sion go by without a party."

Bernie snorted. "Megan considers a broken fingernail
a good enough reason for a party. Hey, maybe she'd
look after Bailey once in a while. Even if she's not ever
going to settle down and have kids of her own, she ought
to get a taste of what parenting's all about." He swung
Bailey off his shoulders. "You'd behave yourself for
Aunt Megan, wouldn't you, punkin?"

Bailey shook her head. "I'm not a punkin, Grampa."

"Well, that's a relief. I thought for a second you
meant you wouldn't be good. Show your mother your
agates."

Bailey held out a fist and slowly unfurled her fingers.
She'd clutched the dozen tiny red-orange stones so
tightly they'd left indentations in her palm. "I like going
to the lake. Aren't they pretty, Mommy?"

"Indeed they are, dear. Let's go put them with your
collection and wash all that sand off you before dinner."

Bailey had never liked having her face washed. It
would be a lot easier, Molly thought, to just put her in
the tub and start from scratch. But Alix wouldn't like to
keep dinner waiting.

She handed Bailey a sliver of soap so the child's
hands would be occupied while she tried to restore some
order to her hair. One ponytail had disintegrated altogether, leaving a pink bow hanging by a couple of curls,

and the other had slid so far it looked more like a cow-lick.

Bernie poked his head around the edge of the door. "I got sent to wash up, too."

Bailey generously handed over her soap.

Molly gave up on the ponytails and settled for combing the tangles out of Bailey's long, fine hair. "Dad, I know you were trying to help, but please don't make Mom feel guilty if she doesn't want to keep Bailey every day. It wouldn't be good for either of them if she feels she's stuck with the job."

"Oh, I don't know. A little guilt now and then's a good thing. But Meditronics has a day-care center right down the street from the administration building."

That would be absolutely ideal, Molly told herself. And yet...

"And if you start taking Bailey there every day," her father said slyly, "I'll bet before long your mother will be pouting and begging to keep her."

Reluctantly, Molly smiled. "Reverse psychology? I won't hold my breath. But if you can come up with as good a plan to get her to quit talking about this divorce business—"

Bernie shook his head. "I think that one's beyond me, sweetheart." He dried his hands, patted Bailey's cheek and headed toward the dining room.

"Mommy." Bailey smoothed the suds over her hands till it looked as if she was wearing white gloves. "What's divorced?"

At least she didn't ask my mother, Molly thought. "It's what happens when two people decide not to be married any more."

Bailey held out her hands to study the effect. "Is that what happened to you and my daddy?"

"Something like that, Bailey. Rinse the soap off now and we'll have dinner—and we'll talk about it later, all right?"

Bailey's lower lip crept out. Molly wasn't sure if the objection was to postponing the conversation or giving up her soap. At the moment, she didn't want to know.

Luke hadn't specified a time for her to come to work the next day, so Molly took her best guess and planned to be in the office by nine. She was almost on her way out of the house when Bailey realized belatedly that she was being left and began to shriek. It took Molly the better part of half an hour to get the child settled down enough to leave her.

By then Alix was tapping her foot and looking impatient, and Molly was not only feeling frazzled, she was longing to point out to her mother that there was an enormous difference between a three-year-old throwing a pure and simple temper tantrum and one who was genuinely miserable at being left behind. Obviously, she wasn't going to have the luxury of even a day to look around for someone to care for Bailey. If there was a spot in the Meditronics facility, she'd better grab it. At least with Bailey just down the street Molly could pop in from time to time.

She was only beginning to breathe freely again when she walked into the main office, but when the secretary who had greeted her the day before looked up with a smile, Molly relaxed.

"Good morning," the secretary said. "I've set up an office for you next door to the conference room, just around that corner. Mr. Luke had some things sent over from the warehouse, but if there's anything special you need—"

"Now that you mention it," Molly began.

The door of the inner office opened and Luke appeared, carrying an open file folder. He laid it on the secretary's desk and, eyes narrowed, studied Molly. "Quite a knack you have—showing up just in time to clock out for lunch."

He sounded genuinely admiring, but Molly wasn't fooled. "I have no plans to leave the building till the end of the day. And in any case, I'm not exactly an employee, remember? I'm a contractor, which means I don't have to punch a time card."

"I suppose not. However, Dad's been here for an hour already."

"Oh. I thought since he was still recuperating…"

"You seem to have inspired him into becoming a morning person." He pushed the folder toward the secretary, but his gaze was on Molly.

He was looking at her as if he couldn't believe his eyes, and Molly wondered if Bailey's tantrum had left her disheveled. By sheer willpower she kept herself from smoothing her palms over her tomato-red skirt. No matter what the reason for that stare, she wasn't going to give him the satisfaction of reacting.

"That's certainly a good indication, isn't it?" she mused. "That he's so eager to start, I mean."

"Don't start spending that bonus just yet," Luke recommended. "Wanda, make sure Ms. Matthews gets an employee badge before she leaves so she doesn't have to go through the routine at the gate every day."

"Yes, sir," the secretary murmured.

"You expect me to give up a daily portrait session?" Molly turned the little laminated card around. "I thought this was much better than yesterday's. And as long as we're on the subject, I was really unhappy when the automated gatekeeper made me give that one back last night before I could leave. What do you use them for, blackmail?"

The secretary, Molly noticed, was trying to fight off a smile.

"It's an idea—though I'll have to work on figuring out what you have that I want." He strode toward his office.

"Luke," Molly said quickly. "I do have a serious question. If I could have a minute in private…?"

"That's just about all I have." He pushed the door open and stood aside for her to precede him.

Molly stopped a few feet inside the door. "There's a little problem of a budget. In addition to the price of my time, putting together a book is going to cost some money. Even if you're assuming it'll never get to the publication stage, there will be certain expenses—"

"We set up a budget. Wanda can get you the precise figures."

"And if your father wants me to pursue my other idea?" She was deliberately nonspecific. He'd had his chance yesterday to explore that avenue, and he hadn't bothered. She wasn't about to make it easy for him. "It won't be inexpensive, either."

"You mean the video version?"

Molly's eyebrows lifted. She had to give him credit for that one. "Curious, were you?"

"Not especially. He rattled on about it all through dinner last night." He glanced at his watch and walked toward his desk. "You'd better hurry," he suggested, "before Dad gets all his joie de vivre back and I conclude you haven't earned anything at all."

Molly fought a sensation of breathlessness and said cheerfully, "Want me to go tell him you've already fired me because you don't care what happens to his book, and then wait and see how long his enthusiasm lasts?"

He tossed a sheaf of papers on the desk blotter. "Dammit, Molly, exactly what do you want?"

"Besides for you to admit you need me just now? Permission to spend some money on the video."

He glared at her. "Put a proposal in writing and have Wanda leave it on my desk."

"Happily," Molly murmured. "Especially the part

about Wanda as delivery person. Goodness knows I don't have any desire to come in here ever again.''

He was still standing by his desk when she walked out, staring after her. Molly knew, because his gaze felt like sandpaper running up and down her spine.

ABOUT FACE

about. *Wanda's thoughts raced*. Goodness knows Ron'll have no desire to come in until late-mor...

He was not standing by the desk when she walked out, leaving her no... Molly knew, because his gaze fell like sunshine on the back of her neck. She...

CHAPTER THREE

MOLLY'S nerves were still vibrating when she reached the office Wanda had indicated, and her first sight of it didn't help. The room was small and almost bare of furniture, but corrugated archival boxes—thirty of them, at least—had been stacked in a ragged half-circle around the desk, taking up most of the floor space. One had been opened. The papers inside were untidy, as if they'd been tossed in rather than filed in order. And the only hint of what the precise contents of each box might be was a date scribbled on the once-white cardboard lid.

Mr. Luke's had some things sent over from the warehouse, Wanda had said. Molly would bet he'd taken great delight in creating this mess. Though it would have been thoughtful of him to have given some consideration to how this sight might affect his father's mood. She'd waded through this kind of chaos before, but for someone who hadn't—someone who wasn't in top condition to start with—the confusion might be overwhelming.

Near the window Warren sat, leafing through what looked like a crumbling scrapbook. He'd shed his coat and tie and rolled up the sleeves of his white shirt. He looked a little overwhelmed, Molly thought, though perhaps that impression arose not so much from Warren himself as the fact that the wall of boxes seemed to be confining him like a prison fence.

"Look here," he said. "It's the original brochure listing products my great-grandfather sold." He held out the scrapbook.

The pages were crackly and the ink faded. The descriptions were fascinating, but the poor quality of the

38

etched illustrations would make them difficult to reproduce. "Somebody went to a lot of trouble to put this scrapbook together."

"It's from the earliest box. Unfortunately, it looks as if nobody had time to look after the later things, and they're a mess." Warren looked perplexed. "I don't know, Molly. This seemed like such a good idea, but now that I see it all spread out..."

"You'll be surprised how quickly we'll be able to make sense of it," Molly said cheerfully. She hoped he didn't suspect that she had her fingers crossed behind her back.

Even with all the clutter, however, and the dust that had her sneezing fiercely and frequently, working with Warren was a joy. The hours sped by, and Molly was surprised when Luke tapped on the office door with a uniformed chauffeur standing behind him.

"Jason was getting worried, Dad," Luke said mildly. "He's been waiting since two o'clock—which is when you told him to pick you up."

"What time is it?" Warren brushed off his fingertips and rolled down his sleeves. Molly noted a streak of grime on the once pristine shirt. "I hadn't noticed."

Molly cast what she intended to be a triumphant look at Luke, and spoiled it with a sneeze.

"God bless you, Molly," Warren said punctiliously. "Though now that you mention it, Lucas, I am feeling a little hungry. What about you, my dear? You've missed your lunch, too. If you'll come with me, I'm sure the cook can find us something."

"Oh—thanks, Warren, it's very sweet of you. But I have some errands to run."

"Of course. I'll see you in the morning, then." He set his hat firmly in place and strolled out, leaning just a little on the chauffeur's arm.

Luke's gaze was like ice. "You just ignored lunch?"

"I didn't intend to," Molly admitted. She felt a little

ashamed of herself for not paying more attention. She should have insisted Warren take a break. "But I'd say we made a good start, wouldn't you?"

Luke surveyed the boxes, now stacked along one wall in a semblance of order, and the desktop, lined with neatly sorted piles. "I told you to inspire him, not work him to death."

"I am sorry about that," she said frankly. "I really did lose track of the time, and I'll be more careful in the future." She took her handbag from the bottom drawer of her desk.

"Are you leaving, too? It's only the middle of the afternoon."

Molly paused in the doorway. "Remember? You said yourself the book isn't my job, Warren is." She smiled at him and snapped off the lights.

Molly was early the next morning—until the automatic gatekeeper refused to acknowledge that she existed. Somewhere inside that emotionless hunk of plastic and metal was the employee badge Wanda had issued her. She'd turned it in as commanded when she'd left the plant at the end of the day, and the machine wouldn't give it back.

She muttered under her breath and tried again, but with an almost threatening buzz the machine said, "Access is denied."

From her safety seat in the back of the car, Bailey commented, "That was a naughty word you said, Mommy."

"It certainly was. And it's a naughty machine, too." A car's horn beeped behind her, and Molly glanced into her mirror. Not only was she blocking traffic, but the black Jaguar waiting in line had pulled so close that she couldn't even get out of the way. It didn't take an Einstein to figure out who was behind the wheel of that sleek, expensive car. "Great," she muttered as she watched Luke get out of the Jaguar.

He strolled up and leaned into her car, his arms folded on the window ledge. "Having a problem?"

"That depends. Have you told the gatekeeper to lock me out?"

"Hadn't thought of it, no."

"Then I don't have a problem, the machine does. I keep typing in my name, but it won't spit out my badge or—more important—open the gate. Perhaps it's gone on strike. How long has it had to work without a day off?"

Luke turned to the keyboard, and moments later the gatekeeper docilely produced Molly's badge. Luke caught it and presented it to her with a tiny bow.

"Stupid machine," she muttered, and hooked the badge onto the collar of her sweater. "Thanks for making me look like a fool. The humans who used to do this job wouldn't have had a problem."

"Oh, I don't know. It seems to be confused about whether you're a regular employee—which puts it in pretty good company, I'd say. On the other hand, it might just not have recognized you with your hair pulled up like that."

Molly's fingertips went to the French braid at the back of her head. "If you think I'm taking my hair down because a machine doesn't approve of the style—"

From the back seat, Bailey piped up. "I need a badge, too."

Molly wanted to groan.

Luke raised his eyebrows, and leaned into the car once more. "Who's this?"

"A very short industrial spy," Molly muttered. "I was hoping to sneak her past you by pretending to enroll her in the day-care center, but of course now that she's blown her cover—"

Luke grinned, but it was Bailey he addressed. "A badge? I think that could be arranged, tyke."

"I'm not a tyke," the child announced with dignity. "I'm Bailey."

"We shouldn't hold up traffic," Molly said. "And whatever she thinks, she doesn't need a badge."

"Well, no—she doesn't. We haven't started labeling all the day-care kids yet. But why shouldn't she have one if she wants?" Luke looked over his shoulder. "There isn't anybody waiting, and it'll only take a minute, anyway. But you'll have to get out of the car, Miss Bailey, to have your picture taken."

Before Molly could object, he lifted the child out of her safety seat and held her up beside the gatekeeper. A couple of minutes later Bailey gleefully showed off her still-warm trophy. The camera had caught her almost in profile, looking at Luke instead of the lens, giggling, with her eyes squeezed almost shut. It was nearly as bad as Molly's first one had been.

"The resemblance between the two of you," Luke said solemnly, "is almost astounding."

"Thank you very much," Molly said. "I suppose when it's time to turn the badge in at the end of the day you'll meet us here and explain why she can't take it home? Because I don't think I can possibly—"

"But she can keep it. It's only a sample, missing all the important coding." He winked at Bailey. "Just in case you really are an industrial spy and intend to flood us with illicit copies." He set her in her seat and stepped away from the car, whistling as he walked to the Jaguar.

Molly shook her head and put the car in gear.

"He's a funny man, Mommy."

"Isn't he, though," Molly muttered. "A regular comedian."

And he'd been practically friendly, too. Which was enough all by itself to make her wonder what the man was up to.

*   *   *

Pure habit was all that guided the Jaguar up the curving main drive to the administration building. Luke pulled the keys from the ignition and sat tapping them on the steering wheel, staring at nothing.

So Molly Matthews had a little girl.

Three years old, maybe? He was no judge of kids' ages—not only did he lack first-hand experience, but he had no particular desire to acquire any. But if he had to take a guess…

So Molly had done exactly as he'd predicted she would. Despite his best efforts, she hadn't learned a thing from her infatuation with him. Angry, frustrated, hurt by what she saw as Luke's rejection, she'd turned to another man to soothe her wounded pride. Obviously not a prizewinner, either, or she wouldn't need this job so desperately. And now she had a child.

Luke carried no guilt for the choices Molly had made, of course. He'd done his best to warn her, to explain how vulnerable she was. But Molly had obviously not been able to see beyond her own nose.

And he certainly felt no satisfaction at being proved correct. He'd done what he thought—what he'd *known*—was right. If, instead, he'd taken advantage of what she'd so trustingly offered him all those years ago…

That little girl might have been mine.

The words were like a jab to his gut, a blow that reminded him of the bruise on Molly' jaw. But he had done what he had to, and apparently so had Molly. And this was no time to start regretting it.

Molly looked over Warren's shoulder at the invoice he'd discovered, folded into a tiny square in a corner of one of the archive boxes. One of the earliest dates they'd found yet, it hadn't been in the earliest of the boxes but with a number of things from a couple of decades later. Just sorting out the mess was shaping up to be a bigger job than Molly had anticipated. After nearly a week they still hadn't opened all the boxes.

Warren's eyes were aglow. "From the date, this must be the first delivery truck my great-grandfather ever owned, and just look what he paid for it. You couldn't buy a bicycle for that these days."

"Not much of a bike, at any rate. Though I'm sure it wasn't inexpensive then." Molly made a note to herself. "In order to compare, we'll need to calculate the average rate of pay in this area at that time. Then we can figure how many hours a person had to work in order to buy—" The phone on the desk rang. "That's probably for you, Warren."

He glanced at his watch. "No doubt it's Jason, and he's early. Tell him I'll be a few minutes yet, will you?"

Molly smiled at him. "You're still spoiled from all the years of having a private secretary." She reached for the phone.

But it wasn't the chauffeur's polite tones that greeted her but a woman's voice saying, "Molly, I need you desperately."

Megan, Molly thought. *Well, there's a first time for everything.* "What's wrong?"

"I'm having a dinner party tonight, and one of my guests called this minute and canceled. So of course I thought of you."

"Because you need an extra woman?" Of course, Molly thought, for Megan that *would* be an emergency. "It's really not a good night for me. By the time I finish here and pick up Bailey and find a sitter—"

"I've already called Mom, and she'll take care of her. Actually, she told me at lunch today that she misses Bailey, can you believe it?"

"Strange, isn't it?" Molly said dryly. *Daddy, the psychologist, was right,* she thought. Of course, he couldn't possibly have lived with Alix for thirty years without figuring out what made her tick.

"Molly, please come."

Molly had to admit to a tinge of curiosity. This might be the only opportunity she'd ever have to get a direct look at how the Bannisters lived. "All right. What time?"

"The guests are invited for seven, but come at six so we can find you a dress."

"I might be able to manage one of my own," Molly said dryly.

"I'm sorry." Megan's voice was small. "I just thought... I'm sorry, Mol."

"It's all right. If Daddy can take Bailey home, I'll come straight there. Otherwise I'll be just as quick as I can."

She thought she heard Megan whisper, "Thanks."

Molly put the phone down with a thoughtful frown. Only when Megan stopped being brittle was it apparent how far from normal she was most of the time.

Molly felt a sudden twinge of guilt because she hadn't tried harder to stay in touch with her sister through the years. But of course Megan hadn't made an effort to maintain contact, either. She hadn't seemed to care, and Molly had had far too much on her mind to worry about it.

Warren's voice brought her back. "Go on and get ready for your party, my dear. You deserve it. I'll sit here and sort a little longer."

"If you're sure... Just don't lift anything heavier than a paper clip, all right?"

Warren smiled. "Don't worry about that. I'm a bit too tired today to be flinging boxes around."

"I'll see you tomorrow, then." Molly picked up her handbag and started down the hall toward her father's office. If Bernie could pick up Bailey tonight...

It was odd, Molly thought, that she suddenly felt so anxious to reach Megan's side.

She popped around a corner and ran headlong into

Luke, who caught her, set her on her feet and stepped out of her way. "Sorry," he said. "If I'd realized what a hurry you were in I'd have gone the other way around."

Molly felt a rush of color in her face. That figured. She'd hardly caught a glimpse of the man since their encounter beside the automatic gatekeeper—so what did she do? Almost trample him, of course. The impact had left her almost breathless, and the muscles in her upper arms, where his hands had rested, were still tingling.

She ignored the sensation and hurried to fill the gap. "I haven't had a chance to tell you how much Bailey loves her badge. She wears it all the time and sleeps with it under her pillow."

"When it wears out let me know."

"You're kidding. Meditronics badges wear out sometimes?"

Luke didn't seem to be listening. His gaze slid from her face down the length of her body. "I know we changed the rules a while back to allow casual dress, but I hardly expected jeans and flannel shirts in the administrative offices."

"Sorry." Molly knew she didn't sound it. "I do try not to run all over the building dressed like this, but it's a purely practical move. That warehouse must not have been dusted since the Roaring Twenties. Come in anytime and dig through a few boxes, and you'll see what I mean. Just don't expect me to wash your shirts afterward." She saw light flare in his eyes, and too late wished she'd put a guard on her tongue.

"Once," he said quietly, "you seemed to want that job."

Molly's breath caught in her throat, and she had to force a smile. "Well, we all have crazy ideas when we're young, don't we? You were right, Luke. You told me that no matter what I thought I couldn't possibly love you, and—obviously—I didn't."

"You were too young and inexperienced to know what love was. That's why I warned you about repeating your mistakes. But you didn't listen, did you, Molly? You plunged straight in anyway. Another man, and then a child—"

She put her chin up a fraction. "If you're implying that Bailey was a mistake, let me assure you that you're dead wrong." She pushed past him.

"And her father?" Luke called after her.

Molly didn't turn around. "What about him?"

"Was he a mistake?"

The question hit her like a knife in the ribs. She clutched at her chest. The silence stretched like taffy.

"Sorry," Luke said. His voice was heavy. "It's not my business."

"It certainly isn't." Molly didn't look back, and she didn't hesitate till she was safely around the next corner. Then she leaned against the wall and sucked in one deep breath after another.

Was he a mistake? "You might say so," Molly muttered. In fact, he'd been the biggest one of her lifetime.

Molly's small car looked pathetically plebeian next to the Bannisters' glass and steel house, perched high atop the bluff overlooking Lake Superior. Molly had never visited the house, though she knew the neighborhood. And Alix had of course sent photographs throughout the two years it had taken to build and decorate the house— so many photographs, in fact, that Molly thought she could probably walk through the place blindfolded.

The pictures hadn't prepared her, though, for the sheer size of the soaring atrium foyer or the trim little blond maid who answered the door. "Mrs. Bannister is in her boudoir," she said. "I'll show you upstairs."

She led the way up a long curved flight of polished black marble steps, down a hallway hushed by the deepest carpet Molly had ever seen, to a closed door, and knocked. Inside, Megan, in an ivory lace peignoir, was taking dresses from a row of closets that lined one wall of the room. She looked distracted. "There's a tangerine-orange thing here somewhere that would look wonderful on you. I bought it before I lightened my hair and—"

"Megan," Molly said firmly. "What is it?"

For a moment, she thought her sister was teetering on the edge of telling her. Then Megan laughed, lightly and unconvincingly, and said, "Oh, you know, some times are better than others. And this is supposed to be one of the good ones." She pulled open another door. "Oh, here it is."

Molly's heart twisted with regret. How she wished they'd been the sort of sisters who could laugh over their triumphs, share their sorrows and be brutally frank with each other when necessary.

As it was, she couldn't force Megan to confide in her. And of course she had to admit that her older sister had never been her first choice of confidante, either.

Megan kept up a steady stream of chatter while Molly showered, then helped her into the silky tangerine dress and stood back for an inspection. "That looks good," she said. "Better than it ever did on me, as a matter of fact. Let's go downstairs, because the guests will be arriving soon. What are you going to wear to Mother and Daddy's anniversary party?"

"I haven't had time to think."

"It's only three weeks off. If you don't want to go shopping, come and rummage through my closets. Of course, if you'd rather go shopping I can tell you all the best places." She led the way down the great staircase and through the atrium and hesitated on the threshold of an enormous living room. She closed her eyes for an instant and took a deep breath, then forced a smile which Molly saw didn't reach her eyes.

"If you hate this so," Molly said, "why do you do it?"

Megan stared at her for an instant, wide-eyed, and then gave a little laugh. "Entertain, you mean? Oh, everybody's nervous right before a party."

Still puzzled, Molly followed her sister into an enormous salon. One end of the room was entirely glass, a dozen huge panes fitted together into a curved wall that provided a stunning panoramic view of the lake far below. Near a white marble fireplace Rand Bannister stood by a black lacquered cart on which a portable bar had been set up, pouring Scotch from a heavy crystal decanter.

Molly hadn't seen him since the wedding, and she regarded him with interest. The years had been kind to Rand, she thought. The young man who had been a bit pompous for Molly's taste seemed to have matured into dignity. His black hair was faintly touched with silver, but his dark good looks still formed a perfect foil for Megan's delicate beauty.

"Molly," he said. "What a surprise to see you."

"Catherine canceled at the last moment," Megan said. "Molly's being a sweetheart and filling in."

"Sweet of her, indeed," he agreed. He added a splash of soda to the glass and handed it to Megan. "Your usual, my dear. And what can I get for you, Molly?"

She accepted a glass of white wine and strolled toward the windows. But the floor-to-ceiling glass was so clear that it seemed nonexistent, and she had a sudden sensation of standing on the edge of a cliff with nothing between her and the lake but a sheer five-hundred-foot drop. Vertigo made her head spin, and she quickly backed away from the windows.

"An incredible view, isn't it?" Rand asked. "I could stand next to that window for hours on end."

Before Molly had to find an answer, the butler spoke

from almost directly behind her, announcing the first couple to arrive.

Molly moved hastily aside, out of the doorway, just as a blond woman in brilliant white swept through. Her flawless skin looked as if she'd been gilded, and Molly wasted a moment speculating how many hours a day she had to spend under a sunlamp to achieve that effect before she let her gaze drift to the woman's escort, standing half a step behind her with his hand resting gently at the small of her back.

Molly's eyes widened, and her heartbeat sped up.

Megan could have warned me, Molly thought, and a second later told herself not to be so silly. Why should she need a warning, after all? Or expect one? Megan had known Luke Hudson forever. Why shouldn't she invite him to dinner?

Luke said, "No wonder you were so anxious to get out of the office today." His gaze flicked over Molly from head to foot, and she saw a gleam in his eyes she thought might have been reluctant approval.

She felt a little glow of warmth and told herself tartly that Luke's evaluation was nothing to get excited about. He probably wasn't admiring her, just the cut of Megan's dress.

"Melinda," he said, "this is Molly Matthews."

The golden girl smiled and held out a hand. "Megan's little sister? What a pleasant surprise to meet you here."

Was there the faintest emphasis on the last word, Molly wondered, or was she only imagining it because she felt so out of place at Megan's party, among Megan's friends?

Melinda went on earnestly, "And may I tell you how much I've always liked that dress? Every time I've seen Megan wearing it, I've meant to tell her."

Well, that removes all doubt about her opinion of me, Molly thought. She manufactured a smile. "Megan has wonderful taste, doesn't she?'' *In everything but her friends,* she wanted to add.

Melinda looked vaguely disappointed at the calm reaction, which made Molly feel a little better—though she was still wondering what had prompted the woman to attack. If it was that casually appraising look Luke had given her… Well, Melinda would have a full-time job if she set out to claw every woman Luke ever glanced at.

The pair moved across the room. Melinda coolly offered her cheek for Rand to kiss, and Luke actually let go of the golden girl long enough to take both of Megan's hands. Molly wondered if he saw the tension she'd noticed in Megan. Was that the slightest trace of a frown on his face as he looked at her?

Another couple arrived a few minutes later, but the last of the guests—a married couple and the single man who was obviously Molly's counterpart—were what she supposed was considered fashionably late. In her opinion, they were just plain rude to keep everyone waiting for more than half an hour.

Of course, she admitted, her judgment was probably affected by the fact that until their arrival she'd felt more like a fifth wheel than an important cog in Megan's dinner party. Or perhaps she was just a bit vexed at the evident disappointment felt by the single man when he realized there'd been a substitution in the guest list. She was almost relieved when Megan asked him to take the golden girl in to dinner, until she realized that left her sitting next to Luke.

By the time they were all seated at Megan's steel and glass dining table, Molly was already eager to call it an evening. She shook out her napkin and tried not to shudder at the sight of the first course.

Luke, beside her, said under his breath, ''You don't need to glare at me. I'm not going to pursue the subject of Bailey and her father.''

"That's a relief," Molly retorted. "But I wasn't glar-
ing at you. Though you needn't take it as a compliment,
on my list of unpleasant things, you aren't anywhere
near as low as oysters on the half shell." She poked at
the offending mollusks. "I'd rather read *Green Eggs and
Ham* twenty-three times in a row than have to sit here
and look at these."

"Relax, they won't last long. What *are* you doing
here, anyway?"

"I thought Megan told you."

He nodded. "Catherine canceled, I know. And now
that I've met the moon-faced gentleman sitting opposite
us I think I can guess why. But—"

"I'm sure he's perfectly nice," Molly said automatically. "So if you mean you're just surprised that Megan
was desperate enough to ask me to fill in—"

He winced. "I wouldn't have put it so crudely,
Molly."

"It hardly matters, it's the truth. And don't ask me
why she called, because I don't know." She hesitated,
half-tempted to ask him what he thought of Megan's
mood tonight. But before she could, the butler returned
to remove the crystal oyster plates and replace them with
bowls of steaming clear broth, and she thought better of
the question.

Across the table, Melinda picked up her soup spoon
and said, "Do you like being back in Duluth, Molly? It
seems a strange choice. But then, I don't suppose someone in your position had a lot of options after your divorce."

If it hadn't been for the earlier remark about Megan's
dress, Molly would probably have ignored the conde-
scension in Melinda's voice. But she'd had just a little
too much of the golden girl tonight, and before she could
stop herself she'd let a faint note of sarcasm creep into
her voice. "Now that you mention it, Melinda, crawling

home and pleading for pity did seem the best of my options.''

Megan hastily broke in and changed the subject, and Molly picked up her soup spoon, noting with detached interest that her fingertips trembled only slightly. She saw, from the corner of her eye, that Luke was frowning. But of course she shouldn't be too surprised at that. She'd have to apologize to Megan, of course.

"If you wouldn't mind, Luke," she said softly, "I'd appreciate it if you'd take Melinda out on the terrace after dinner—" *and drop her in the lake* "—and assure her that she can safely stop taking potshots because she doesn't have a thing to fear from me."

"You know," Luke said thoughtfully, "I'm not so sure I agree with you."

For a moment Molly wasn't certain she'd heard him correctly, and her breath caught painfully in her throat. Could he mean that he truly thought Melinda had a reason to run scared of her? Of plain old Molly Matthews? If so, that could only mean that Luke really had been…intrigued by her, perhaps? Impressed? Attracted? Every nerve in her body tingled. She felt half-frightened, half-excited, as if without thought she'd embarked on a new and scary carnival ride and it was now too late to get off.

"If cattiness was a world-class poker game," he mused, "I'd say you beat her pair of insults with a very nicely played humiliation."

The electrical thrumming of her nerves died till only an occasional spark jerked through her body. How stupid could she be, assuming that he thought she was any real competition for the glamorous Melinda! Of course he didn't.

And why should you care what he thinks? she asked herself.

She hardly noticed the rest of the dinner. Courses came and went, and the conversation shifted from art to politics to people Molly had never met. Eventually, however, the butler served chocolate mousse and started to pour coffee, and Molly tried to smother a sigh of relief. Just a little longer, she told herself, and she could make her escape.

The maid who had greeted Molly at the door that afternoon came into the dining room and whispered something to the butler. He frowned and leaned over Luke's shoulder, and Molly heard him murmur, "A telephone call for you, sir. It seems to be quite important."

Luke pushed his chair back. He was almost clumsy in his haste. His chest brushed Molly's bare shoulder as he rose, sending a quiver of heat through her. "Excuse me, please."

The golden girl said, "What is it, Lucas? In the middle of a dinner party, I should think you—"

Luke shook his head and followed the maid from the room. When he came back a couple of minutes later, he looked pale, and foreboding clutched at Molly's heart.

"It's my father," he said. "He's had a relapse, and they're taking him to the hospital. I'm sorry, Megan, but I'll have to go."

"Good heavens, Luke," Megan said, "don't you dare apologize!" Her voice was low and almost shaky, and fondness stirred in Molly's heart. Perhaps inside that fragile shell there was still a woman worth knowing, after all.

"Someone will make sure Melinda gets home," Rand said. "There's no need for her to go now and miss out on chocolate mousse."

After all, the mousse is so much more important than Warren being ill, Molly thought. But of course Rand hadn't meant it that way. He'd just been trying to reassure Luke.

She felt half sick. What was it Warren had said this afternoon as she was saying goodbye? *I'm a bit too tired today to be flinging boxes around,* that was it. Had he been feeling ill and refused to admit it?

And what, exactly, did "relapse" mean? She supposed it could be anything from a feeling of weakness to another stroke.

And she wondered—and felt disloyal for even thinking about it, when Warren might be fighting for his life—where this would leave his beloved book project...and Molly herself.

Her own words came back to her in a haunted echo. *The book's not my job,* she'd told Luke. *Warren is.*

So what would happen now?

CHAPTER FOUR

MOLLY noticed that Melinda daintily spooned up every bit of her chocolate mousse, but the rest of them didn't have much appetite, and the party broke up not long after Luke left.

Molly fought a losing battle with her conscience and finally offered Melinda a ride. But the golden girl flashed a smile at Rand and said, "Oh, can't I have a run in your new Mercedes instead, Rand? And I'm sure Molly and Megan are longing to have a good chat—they seem to find so few chances to talk."

Molly bit her tongue till after they were gone. "No doubt she would have picked up some sort of infection from my car.... I'm really sorry I snapped at her over dinner, though."

Megan shrugged. "Don't worry. I've done it myself."

Then why do you have her around? Molly wanted to ask.

"Some women are just like that." Megan's voice was flat. "Needing all the masculine attention in the room and with no time at all for other women."

Molly felt alarmed at the lifeless tone. "You're exhausted. Can I help you up to bed? Maybe call the maid?"

Megan shook her head. "Just sit with me a while, will you?"

"Well, I can't stay long. I have to go to work tomorrow." Until she heard otherwise... No, that was defeatist thinking—assuming the worst. She'd just pretend Warren was vacationing for a few days, and she'd work like fury so she'd have something wonderful to show him when he got back.

Unless Luke told her not to bother.

"Just when I thought I could see a light at the end of the tunnel," Molly mused, "this happens."

"Funny you should put it that way." Megan let her head drop against the brocade chair. "I was thinking just about the same thing myself."

Molly sat very still, afraid that if she moved her sister might once more dance away from the subject.

With a short and entirely humorless laugh, Megan said, "I'm pregnant."

Molly was stunned. There was no joy in her sister's voice, no glow in her eyes, no wonder in her face. *This is supposed to be one of the good times,* she had said.

"Do you want to be?" Molly asked bluntly.

"I don't know." Megan didn't meet her eyes. "Do me a favor, all right? Don't tell Mother."

"You haven't told *Mother?*" The words were out before Molly could stop herself. "Sorry. Not my business." When the silence became unbearable, she moved from her chair to kneel next to Megan's. Her sister's hands were cold and almost limp. Molly held them between hers. "I know how it feels to be pregnant and scared. And I'm here for you, Meg. Anytime you want me."

Megan's eyes pooled with tears. "Even though I wasn't there for you?"

"That was a long time ago."

Megan wet her lips. "Thanks, Mol. I'll remember. I think I can sleep now."

Molly waited till Megan had climbed the stairs before she let herself out the front door and went to her car.

Megan pregnant. And drinking Scotch and soda. She'd had a glass in her hand most of the evening. Though it had been a full glass, Molly recalled, so maybe she'd only been holding it, not drinking. But surely Rand wouldn't have poured alcohol for her if...

Had she even told Rand yet? Even if she hadn't, Molly reminded herself, it didn't mean there was anything sinister going on. Maybe there hadn't been an opportunity. However, if Megan hadn't insisted on Molly coming early, she'd have had plenty of time before dinner tonight.

Maybe that was what was wrong, she thought—if there was a reason Megan didn't want to tell him. Maybe he didn't want a child. Or maybe it wasn't his child.

"And you," Molly told herself rudely, "could start writing for the soap operas any day!"

Well, she'd done all she could for now. She couldn't turn Megan upside down and shake her till the truth fell out, no matter how much she'd like to.

She took the long way home so she could drive down London Road past Warren Hudson's house. It would be more accurate to call Oakwood an estate, she supposed, for the property stretched over several acres and to the lakefront. The house lay well back from the street, sheltered by so many trees that she could barely see the gleam of moonlight on brick walls and tile roof. The windows were dark except for a couple of lights toward the back, where the servants' quarters were. It looked like a house at peace, settled down for the night, but Molly knew better. It was a house waiting, breath held, for news.

She tried not to remember the set, drained look on Luke's face when he'd gotten the news. She'd seen him looking like that once, on the night before his mother had died.

But the similarity of expression didn't mean, necessarily, that Warren was in grave danger—only that Luke was afraid. As of course he would be, getting the news like that. Perhaps, by the time he'd reached his father's side, the medical report had been better than he'd expected it would be.

Molly wished she knew which hospital they'd taken Warren to. Not that she'd rush straight over to console Luke, of course. It was hardly her place to do that, though the thought of him sitting there alone made her heart shiver.

Wasn't it a bit odd that the golden girl hadn't insisted on rushing out with him? Of course, the fact that they'd arrived at the party together didn't mean they were seriously involved. And though Melinda hadn't hesitated to show her claws the instant Luke paid attention to Molly, she hadn't seemed to mind at all when he'd departed so suddenly. Maybe Megan was right and the golden girl would have reacted the same way if it had been another man—Rand, even—instead of Luke who'd dared to notice Molly. And Luke hadn't apologized to Melinda for stranding her, just to Megan for breaking up the party.

It was a shame, actually, if they weren't involved— because Molly would find great humor in the idea of Luke being spellbound by a woman who saw him as no more than a convenient accessory. That sort of treatment would be no more than he deserved. There had been a time, after all, when Molly would have been thrilled to have even that much notice from Luke. Instead, he'd viewed her as a damned nuisance.

At the Matthews house, lights blazed from the living room where her parents were playing bridge with another couple. George and Jessie, Molly recalled. She'd met them last week. Or was it Jesse and Georgia?

Molly's father tossed down his cards when he saw her. "Now I know why I'm fighting off yawns," he said. "If Megan's party has already broken up, it's past time for my old bones to be in bed."

"But it's not all that late," Alix said. Her gaze focused suspiciously on Molly.

I didn't disgrace myself, Mother, and I wasn't asked to leave, she wanted to say. Instead, she told them the little she knew about Warren's setback.

Bernie shook his head. Molly got the impression he wasn't shocked or even startled—just sad. She wondered if she was the only one who'd been convinced Warren was getting better by the day.

"Anyway," she went on, "nobody felt much like celebrating, and Megan was tired, so we all left."

"I've never known Megan to be worn out," Jessie said. "The girl's inexhaustible. Of course, we could all keep going forever if we had Rand's resources to draw on."

Molly said carefully, "She seemed to have something on her mind." She wouldn't tell her mother about Megan's secret—but surely, if Alix had a hint that all wasn't well, she would be more alert to Megan's needs.

"Trouble with her hairdresser, I suppose," Jessie said with a laugh. "It couldn't be much more. With the tub of money she fell into, Megan's got nothing to worry about for the rest of her life." She played her last card triumphantly. "Not like you, Molly, dear. And poor little Bailey—losing her father like that."

Molly shot a look at her mother.

"Bad enough that your marriage didn't work out," Jessie went on, "but then for him to die like that so you're not even getting child support—"

Alix had turned pink. She swept up the deck of cards and said, "Another drink, anyone? Hot cider?"

Molly said, "Sounds great. I'll help you, Mom." In the kitchen, she glanced over her shoulder to be certain they were alone. "And what was *that* all about?"

Alix shrugged. "Darling, the man never visits his daughter, he doesn't help you with money... I have to explain your situation somehow."

"You don't have to explain anything," Molly said grimly. "But I know better than to think you'll stop—

so in the future will you at least warn me of the twists in the plot?''

Alix bit her lip.

''I'm going to check on Bailey,'' Molly announced. ''Tell your friends good-night for me, will you?''

She tiptoed into the smallest bedroom, the one she had occupied as a child. Bailey was sprawled on top of the blankets, her neck bent at an awkward angle, her face smashed firmly into her pillow. Molly straightened and covered her, and marveled at the way the child was growing. Though she'd always been small for her age, Bailey was obviously starting into a growth spurt. She'd need an entirely new wardrobe before long.

Molly rubbed her temples. It was all very well to tell herself not to borrow trouble. But she hadn't sought out tonight's whole truckload of worries, it had been dumped on her. As if Warren's relapse wasn't enough, there was Megan's pregnancy. And just to top things off, her mother had blithely killed off her inconvenient ex-husband.

Something had to give. Molly just hoped it wouldn't be her.

As she climbed the front steps of the Hudson mansion a couple of days later, Molly squared her shoulders and tried to fight off a sense of déjà vu.

This visit wasn't truly a repetition, of course. The other time she'd found herself standing on Oakwood's doorstep on a visit of sympathy, it had been a chilly, damp October evening. Luke's mother had still been fighting her futile battle against the virulent cancer that had killed her, and Molly had been sent to deliver a basket of flowers from her parents.

This time it was full daylight, though the sun was dropping rapidly and was no longer producing much warmth. She'd tucked a gaily wrapped compact disk under her arm, and Bailey was tugging impatiently at her hand.

"This is a *big* house. Will we go in? Can I ring the doorbell, Mommy?"

"Yes, you may ring the bell, and no, I don't think we'll be going inside." But the child couldn't reach high enough, so Molly lifted her so she could press the ornate button, then stooped to make one last hopeless effort to brush the streaks of dirt off the child's pastel jacket. "At least your face is clean," she muttered. "But of all the days for the day-care center to take a field trip to the zoo..."

The door opened behind Molly, and Bailey leaned to one side of her mother so she could peer into the house. For an instant, as if in a dream, time seemed to fold back on itself. Molly half expected to turn around and look up at Watkins the butler and see, as she had that night so long ago, that his usually impassive face was tight with worry.

The change in him that October night had startled her out of her planned speech. Instead of the pretty words telling how sad her parents were about Isabel Hudson's struggle, she'd heard herself say in little more than a whisper, "Is Luke here?"

Watkins had stared at her for a long moment and then said, "Yes, miss. He went out to the garden some time ago to be by himself." His voice steadied. "But I'm not sure he should be alone right now. I believe he's sitting in the treehouse."

The treehouse...

Molly wondered if it was still there, perched in the huge old maple tree halfway between the house and the lake. Surely not, after all these years without a child around to use it.

Though Luke hadn't been a child when his mother lay dying and he'd looked for solace there.

A deep voice, very unlike Watkins's, said, "If you want to see my father—"

Luke. She hadn't expected him to be answering the door. Hastily Molly straightened and faced him. "No, I didn't intend to disturb him on his first day at home— or you, either. I just stopped by on my way from work to drop off a little gift. Perhaps you'd give him this?" She held out the small square package.

Luke showed no inclination to take it.

"You don't need to act as if it's poisonous," Molly said impatiently. "In fact, unlike candy, it's nonfattening and cholesterol-free, and unlike flowers, it's guaranteed not to set off hay fever. And it's not even depressing— I chose the music very carefully. I'd think you'd realize I'm the last person who'd want to do Warren any harm just now."

Luke rubbed a hand across the back of his neck. "Sorry. It's been a long couple of days." He reached for the package.

Molly was instantly contrite. She knew perfectly well he hadn't set foot in the office since Warren's relapse, and she wouldn't be surprised to find that he hadn't left the hospital at all. "And I'm sure the nights were longer yet," she said gently.

"I don't know. Time all blurred together somehow— sort of like it used to in med school."

Bailey took a step toward Luke, dug a small hand into the back pocket of her blue jeans and held up a plastic rectangle, its edges sadly frayed. "I still have my badge," she announced.

"It looks a bit the worse for wear," Luke said.

"That's 'cause Joey took it at day care. The teacher made him give it back, but he bent it all up. He's mean sometimes."

"Bailey, don't pester Mr. Hudson. He's very tired just now."

Bailey studied him, her tiny nose wrinkled thoughtfully. "Then you have to take a nap."

"Life's so simple when you're not quite four," Molly said. "But it's not bad advice, anyway."

Luke smiled slowly. "Thanks, Molly. I'll give this to Dad and tell him—"

From the dim hallway behind him, Warren said, "You'll tell Dad what?" He came into view, moving slowly, leaning on a walker. "Hello, Molly. Did Lucas tell you I wanted to talk to you?"

She flashed a glance at Luke. He looked a little guilty, she thought as he stood aside for her to enter. But she couldn't exactly blame him—Warren looked like a pale shadow of the man he'd been just a few days ago, and hardly up to having visitors.

As she stepped across the threshold into Oakwood, Molly automatically reached for Bailey's hand. But the child slipped away from her and moved three steps into the hallway, with its parquet floor and linen-fold paneling, where she stood stockstill and stared up the long, wide, straight, golden oak staircase to the first landing, almost as large as a room. Her eyes had gone wide. Molly wasn't surprised. Lots of people had that sort of reaction to this house.

Certain that Bailey was too awed to move, she turned her attention once more to Warren. "You know," she said mildly, "if all you wanted to do is talk to me, it really wasn't necessary to create all this fuss. You could have just asked me to stick around and chat the other day."

Warren smiled weakly—about all the reaction the feeble joke was worth, Molly admitted—and sank down on the bench at the foot of the stairs. "Pardon me, but I think I'd better rest a bit before I go up."

Molly was horrified. "You aren't going to try to walk up, are you?"

"No, I'll just go as far as the elevator, for today."

Bailey had slowly turned a full circle, inspecting the hallway. Now she focused on Warren's walker. "What's that, Mommy?"

"It's to help Mr. Hudson get around the house, dear."

Bailey frowned. "Why did you call him Mr. Hudson?"

"Because that's his name." Molly saw the child's puzzled gaze shift from Warren to Luke, and added hastily, "Both of them are Mr. Hudson."

Bailey obviously thought that made no sense at all, but she politely turned her attention to the walker. "Did you break your leg?" she asked earnestly. "When my mommy fell down the stairs and broke her leg she used crutches."

Warren shook his head. "I'm sick in a different way, but it's still hard for me to walk."

"When I'm sick," Bailey confided, "I have to stay in bed."

Molly's patience had vanished. "Bailey, I don't think your contributions to the conversation are quite—"

Through a door at the shadowed back of the hall came a large dog, her red-gold coat gleaming, her head up, nose twitching, toenails clicking against the parquet floor. She trotted straight to Bailey and sniffed at the child's face, almost on the level with her own.

Bailey giggled and threw her arms around the dog's neck.

Before Molly could move, Luke had caught the animal's collar. "Lucky's pretty much kid-proof," he said, "but just in case…"

The dog swiped her tongue across Bailey's face, and the child shrieked with laughter.

Molly thought she saw the shadow of pain cross Warren's face at the noise. "I'm sorry," she said. "If you want to talk to me, Warren, I can stop in the morning after I've taken Bailey to day care. I shouldn't have brought her with me today."

Warren shook his head, but she thought it was no more than a polite protest.

Luke obviously thought so, too, for he released the dog's collar and stood up. "Bailey, let's take Lucky out for a bit. I'll show you how to make her do tricks."

As the door swung shut behind the trio, Molly said, "So much for asking permission." She sat beside Warren. "So what do the doctors say?"

"Just that I've been overdoing it."

"It wasn't another stroke, then?"

Warren shook his head. "My blood pressure went way up the other night, till they thought I was likely to have one. Then it dropped to the vanishing point, and that didn't make them happy, either. Damned doctors," he grumbled. "You can't please them no matter what you do."

Molly smothered a smile. "It isn't fair of them to keep changing the rules, is it?"

"So they tell me I have to slow down, and nobody has any idea how long it'll be before I can do anything productive again. If ever." His voice was heavy, almost lifeless. Then he cleared his throat and said with determination, "But the project must go on. You'll have to handle it by yourself, of course, but I want you to know that I have complete faith—"

The project must go on. *Fat chance of that,* Molly thought. As soon as Luke realized that his father couldn't be involved any more...

But it had been Warren's mental state Luke had seemed most interested in, not the physical work he'd been doing. And Warren was obviously still interested, so surely he could still play some part in the whole process.

It was not, however, the possibility of preserving her job which prompted her to say, "It wouldn't be the same without you. I need you to bounce ideas off, and to give me background and context. Could you spare energy for that if I stopped by now and then to show you the pieces I'm working on?"

A faint light sprang to life in Warren's eyes, but he shook his head. "It'd be a lot of trouble for you—driving back and forth, dragging things over here."

As a matter of fact, Molly admitted to herself, it would be a bit of a pain. But she'd put up with a lot more inconvenience than that if it would help Warren. "It wouldn't even be out of my way. I could just stop by on my way home from work."

With Bailey in tow? Hardly.

But, she reminded herself, the whole reason for working at the plant had been Warren. Now she could be much more flexible.

He seemed to have read her mind. "Maybe you could work here instead. There's plenty of room. We could have all the archives moved, and set up a little office for you—"

And why not? Molly asked herself. Of course Warren's doctors didn't want him to overdo, but she suspected it wasn't the work that had exhausted him but the way he'd gone about it. She could see it as she looked over the week they'd worked together. He'd only missed lunch that one time—but though he'd never said so, Warren had obviously felt that if he'd gone to the effort to get dressed and have Jason drive him across Duluth to the plant he should stay half a day, at least.

But if she moved a minimal office into Oakwood, Warren could work precisely when he felt like it, in ten-minute stretches if he wanted. He wouldn't even have to get out of bed.

"I'll talk to Luke about the idea," she said.

Warren snorted. "What's it got to do with him? This isn't Luke's house, it's still mine—and I can do what I please with it. Besides, you're working for me, so what's it to him where you put your desk? I'll expect you in the morning." He pushed himself up from the bench. "Watkins!"

The butler appeared silently. "Yes, sir?"

"Help me up to my room, will you? And that small bedroom next to mine—I want you to put a desk in there, and a couple of tables."

His voice faded as he trudged down the hallway. Molly watched as the butler opened what appeared to be a closet door and helped Warren step inside. A moment later the elevator's whir emphasized that she'd been dismissed.

She shook her head and turned toward the back of the house, the direction she figured Luke and Bailey and the dog had gone.

The hallway led past a well-equipped butler's pantry and into the kitchen where a woman with rosy, plump cheeks was cleaning vegetables.

"Sorry to intrude," Molly said. "But I'm looking for my little girl, and I thought perhaps…"

"They went on out to the garden," the cook said.

The words echoed faintly in Molly's mind. *He went out to the garden to be by himself,* Watkins had told her on that long-ago night. And today, tired and worn, Luke would probably have enjoyed the same sort of solitude. Instead, she'd unintentionally saddled him with an active three-year-old. "Thanks," she said, and hurried to the back door.

From the narrow porch she could hear Bailey, and she followed the sound of high-pitched giggles through the garden, where crocus and daffodils were just coming to life, and down a winding path toward the lake.

She found Luke sitting on a wrought-iron bench at the farthest corner of the formal garden, where between the trees she could just catch the glimmer of water.

Bailey knelt nearby, her arms around the dog's neck. "I like the lake," she announced as Molly came within earshot. "Can I go down by the water?"

"Not today," Luke said. "I might take you sometime, though."

"Not even if Lucky goes?"

Luke didn't answer. He started to rise when he saw Molly, but she shook her head and he sank onto the bench.

The dog pulled free and edged in front of Bailey, eyes intent on Molly.

"Lucky," Luke warned. "You don't need to protect the kid from her mother, so knock it off."

Molly sat next to him. "I see they've become the best of buddies."

Lucky settled onto her haunches, knocking Bailey off balance. The child sat down hard and rolled onto her back. "What's that?" she asked, pointing into a big tree beyond the edge of the formal garden.

Luke didn't even turn his head. "A treehouse," he said.

Molly's throat tightened. Despite her best intentions of ignoring the treehouse, the reminder made her look up.

The treehouse was no rustic boys' hideaway slapped together from odd boards. It was an actual tiny cabin, which happened to be located twenty feet above the ground in the spreading branches of an ancient maple. The dark green paint was chipping, and the windows looked as if they hadn't been cleaned in years. But the door was solid, the shingles all in place, the glass unbroken—so she was certain the inside would still be dry. Dusty, perhaps, and cold from long disuse, and smelling a bit stale...

Just as it had been that October night when she'd found Luke sitting there, staring at nothing.

Bailey was still sprawled on her back staring at the tree. "Who lives up there?"

"Nobody," Luke said.

"Why not?"

"Stop pestering, Bailey. Mr. Hudson's very tired."

"His name's Luke," Bailey informed her. "He told me so."

Molly asked, "You don't mind if she calls you that?" But she forgot her question as she took her first really good look at Luke. In the shadow of the front portico, in the dimness of the house, he'd looked tired. But now, in the sunlight, she could see that his eyes were red-rimmed and his face was haggard. "This is ridiculous," she said. "We're going home, and you're going to rest. In fact, come to think of it...have you bothered to eat?"

Luke rubbed a hand over his jaw. "Not lately, that I remember."

"At least we can do something about that. Don't move, I'll be right back. Bailey, come with me. You can charm the cook, and Mr. Hudson—Luke—doesn't need to look after you any more."

Lucky protested the abrupt loss of her playmate and only settled after a stern word from Luke.

A few minutes later, when they returned with a basket, Luke had leaned his head against the back of the bench and closed his eyes. *Sound asleep,* Molly thought, but it was too late to hush Bailey. She broke free and raced down the path, calling, "Treats! We brought treats!"

Luke opened his eyes. "Judging from the size of that basket, Molly, I'd say you were right about her being able to con the cook."

"I said charm, not con." Molly dug into the basket. "A cookie for Bailey—"

Bailey grinned and tried to hold the enormous round of chocolate-chip cookie safely above the dog's head.

Molly added hastily, "And a rawhide chew for Lucky." She tossed it to the dog and sat on the bench once more, the basket between her and Luke. "And the rest is for you. The cook was a bit defensive—she said she'd tried twice since you came home to feed you. So

I think you'd better eat every crumb if you expect her to speak to you ever again."

He picked up a foil-wrapped sandwich. "You seem to always be taking care of me, Molly. Not always the same way, but—"

Molly tried to will herself not to tense, but the effort was in vain. She stared straight ahead, but she wasn't seeing Oakwood's gardens but the inside of that cold, silent treehouse on a chilly night in October. The night she had asked Luke to make love to her.

He pressed two fingers to the center of his forehead. "I'm sorry. That was…"

She forced herself to smile. "You're worn out."

"I'm a clumsy fool. But since the subject's been raised—and since you're all grown up now and obviously over that crush you had on me—"

"No question about that," Molly said crisply.

"I might as well confess that sending you away that night was one of the tougher things I've ever done."

"Really? You sounded as if you enjoyed telling me to get lost."

"I had to—or I couldn't have managed to pull it off. If you'd stayed another minute—"

Another minute, Molly thought, *and my life would be completely different today.*

His voice was little more than a whisper. "You were so very, very sweet that night.…"

She knew he'd leaned closer, but she kept her gaze fixed on Bailey, who was quietly feeding the crumbs of her cookie to the dog. His fingertips came to rest on the nape of her neck, four small spots, which functioned like electrical connections, sending jolts of current through her skin, urging her to turn her head to look at him.

She closed her eyes and fixed her will on denying that impulse. The man was exhausted, she told herself. He hardly knew what he was saying, and as for kissing her…she knew very well they'd both regret that.

But why? a little voice whispered deep in her mind. *What's such a big deal about a kiss of gratitude? You're over him. You've been done with that stupid crush for years. He just wants to thank you....*

Luke's lips brushed the line of her jaw, precisely on the faded spot where the bruise had been. "So sweet," he whispered again, and raised his other hand to her chin and turned her face toward his.

She stared into his eyes, far darker than their usual hazel tones, and tried to tell herself that there would be nothing remarkable about this kiss. It was just a different way to say thanks....

She didn't remember moving, but an instant later she was standing on the path in front of the bench, holding out a hand to Bailey. "Come on, honey, and say good-bye to the dog. We need to get home."

"Running away?" Luke asked. His voice was low, almost husky.

Molly didn't look at him. "Avoiding unpleasantness."

But she knew she wasn't telling the truth. She had pulled away not because she expected his kiss to be distasteful—but because she hadn't wanted him to kiss her in gratitude.

And she also knew that if he had, she wouldn't have wanted him to stop.

CHAPTER FIVE

As THE butler set a steaming waffle before him and refilled his coffee cup, Luke folded the newspaper and laid it aside. "Is my father awake yet, Watkins?"

"Yes, sir. He's having breakfast in his room, though. He said something about reserving his energy for later, when he might need it."

Luke frowned as he cut into the waffle. Warren was taking it easy, looking after himself—exactly as he should. *So why do I have such a negative feeling about it?*

And what did he mean, reserving energy in case he needed it later? It was perfectly fine to be cautious, but if Warren started treating himself like spun sugar candy...

That, Luke thought gloomily, was just about where the trouble had started before, right after the stroke. Uncertain of what he could safely do in the present, Warren had retreated to the past. But the cure Luke thought he'd found for that particular difficulty had turned out to be almost as bad as the problem. Now he not only had his father's frail health to be concerned about, but he was stuck with an expensive project to record the company's history....

Though in fact he *wasn't* boxed in. He could call a halt any time, for there'd been no contract signed between Molly Matthews and Meditronics.

Major oversight on her part, Luke thought, *not to insist on one.* Or perhaps it was just one more indication of how badly she'd needed this job...

Maybe Molly would have some insights on handling

73

Warren. He'd ask her as soon as he got to work. Not that there was any point in hurrying to the plant. He was already setting an all-time record for lateness after his first sleep in longer than he cared to think about. So he might as well enjoy his breakfast.

Automatically, he cut another bite from his waffle.

Molly. She'd been so gentle with Warren yesterday. Without minimizing the severity of his illness, she'd still managed to encourage him to find humor in the situation. And she'd been concerned about Luke, as well—distressed by his lack of sleep, worried about whether he ate.

Right up to the moment when, in response to that warmth, he'd tried to kiss her. Just a simple kiss, the sort of thing every other woman he knew exchanged at the drop of a greeting—but Molly had flash frozen.

Why hadn't she let him kiss her? She'd wanted to—he couldn't be wrong about that. When he'd first turned her face toward him, her eyes had been great dark pools flooded with desire. And then, within a millisecond, instead of a warm and willing woman, there'd been an iceberg in his arms. Or, rather, *not* in his arms. He still wasn't quite sure how she'd slipped away. Of course, he hadn't been holding her so tightly that she couldn't move. That had never been Luke's style. But his reflexes should have been fast enough to counter whatever it was that had so suddenly changed her mind and at least try to change it back.

The part that really annoyed him, he concluded, was not knowing what had caused that sudden transformation.

Nothing he'd done, that was sure. She hadn't shied from his touch. She'd known perfectly well he intended to kiss her, and at first she'd been more than willing. So what might she have seen, or thought, or remembered, which had prompted her behavior?

The fact that her daughter was there? Possible, he

thought, but not very likely. The child must have seen casual kisses before—and maybe not-so-casual ones, too.

And surely that sudden freeze hadn't been caused by a stray feeling of loyalty to the ex-husband, either. That marriage had obviously been over with long ago, so long that there wasn't even a hint of an indentation at the base of Molly's finger where a wedding ring would have rested. After so much time…

Wait a minute, he thought. If she'd been divorced long enough for all traces of a ring to vanish, who had put that bruise on her jaw just a couple of weeks ago?

But a divorce didn't put the ex-husband out of the running entirely, he realized. There would still have to be contact when there was a child involved. If the ex had come to see Bailey and gotten angry at her mother…

If he ever tries it again, he thought grimly, *I hope I'm there to make sure he finds out what it feels like to get a solid fist in his face.*

Whatever had happened between her parents, though, it hadn't seemed to leave a mark on Bailey. Molly was doing a good job there. He couldn't remember seeing a child take more pleasure in simple things than Bailey had yesterday, romping with Lucky, sharing her cookie, giggling in delight. She'd even given him an unprompted hug to say goodbye—a gesture of affection that had touched his heart—while her mother had refused even to look him in the eye because he'd tried to steal a kiss.

Which pretty much brought him right back to where he'd started. Except that now his waffle was cold.

He noted the sound of the doorbell, but when a moment later Watkins's footsteps sounded on the parquet floor of the hall he dismissed it from his mind. Another delivery of flowers, no doubt—it was a bit early for any of Warren's friends to be stopping by to visit.

It was only when he heard the muted sound of a feminine voice in the hall that he paid attention. At first he thought it was Megan Bannister, but Megan's husky tones were the product of years of practice. This voice was softer and even more sultry—and he'd bet his next set of stock options that its owner had no idea how sexy it was. But what was Molly doing here in the middle of the morning?

He didn't make a conscious decision to push his plate aside and investigate. He was in the hallway before he realized he'd moved.

She was just inside the front door, handing a brown suede jacket to Watkins. She certainly didn't dress like a woman in need of a job, Luke thought. No jeans to-day—which was something of a pity, actually. When a woman had legs as long and slim as Molly's were... Of course, she looked good in that narrow silky skirt, too, even though it covered up more than he'd like.

She stooped to retrieve her briefcase and spoke to the butler. "There are some boxes in my car. I'd appreciate it if someone could bring them in."

Luke stepped forward. "Thank you, Watkins. That's all."

He saw the instant flare of fear in Molly's eyes, and annoyance washed over him. What was the matter with the woman? It had only been a kiss, and he could take a hint. After the message he'd gotten yesterday, he was hardly likely to throw her on the floor and...what was that wonderful Victorian phrase? Oh, yes, have his way with her.

Even if the idea did sound inviting.

The door of the butler's pantry shut behind Watkins, and Luke said, "Boxes? What are you doing, moving in?"

"Didn't your father tell you?"

No wonder, he thought, that Warren was still in bed this morning, reserving his strength! "There wasn't much time," he admitted. "We were both pretty busy sleeping last night."

"I'm sorry, because I meant to tell you yesterday. What Warren and I talked about, I mean."

"I can't imagine," he drawled, "what would have made you forget."

She turned a delicious shade of pink. At least, Luke thought, fear wasn't the only emotion in her mind when she recalled that aborted kiss. He remembered the instant yesterday when she'd been looking forward to his caress, and he wondered how difficult it would be to make her look at him that way again.

"I've been to the plant this morning," she said, "and I brought a couple of boxes over to work on here."

"Determined, aren't you?"

"To keep my word, yes. Look, it wasn't my idea to move my office over here, but what difference does it make where I work?"

"Oh, it's just the *office* you're moving," he murmured.

"You can't honestly think Warren suggested I *live* here?"

"The place does have its advantages. Tennis court, swimming pool, full-time staff…"

"Well, he didn't. And since I intended in the first place to do the bulk of my work at home, what's the big deal about bringing it here? That way Warren can be as involved as he wants, do what he's able to and still get all the rest he needs."

Despite the way she'd raised her chin the fraction of an inch, Luke thought he could hear the slightest trace of a quaver in her voice. "I'm not going to argue with you about it, Molly." He took a step closer and realized that her lower lip was trembling slightly.

"Does that mean you've already made up your mind? Even with this setback, Warren hasn't given up. Why should you be in a hurry to sacrifice the whole idea?"

"Who said I was giving up?"

She hesitated. "Then I still have a job?"

Luke nodded. He watched the sleek line of her throat and saw the convulsive ripple of muscles as she swallowed hard.

And he wondered if that meant she was relieved, or if she understood he hadn't just been talking about her job.

Now that it was far too late, Molly knew she should have just let him kiss her in the garden yesterday, because that would have been the end of it. One quick, simple kiss. But no—she'd had to make a challenge out of it, and now his interest was piqued. Or at least he wanted her to think it was, just for the fun of keeping her off balance. Either way, she'd have to watch her step more closely than before.

She watched as he strolled across the hallway and went out the front door without a backward glance, and she released a tiny sigh of relief as the latch clicked. With any luck, she wouldn't catch another glimpse of him all day.

She looked up the long staircase with a frown. She could hardly start by wandering around upstairs looking from room to room for an office that might not even be set up yet.

A soft voice pulled her attention to the main floor, to a small woman dressed in black who had quietly approached. "Miss Matthews? I'm Hilda Ekberg, the housekeeper. Mr. Warren asked me to show you upstairs and to get you anything you might want."

Molly smiled. "He might regret giving me quite so much latitude."

The housekeeper's gaze was unexpectedly shrewd. Molly felt almost as if she was being turned inside out for inspection. "Oh, I'm sure he knows exactly what he's doing." She led the way up the long stairs and turned toward the back of the house.

"He mentioned the bedroom next to his," Molly said.

"I'll do my best to be quiet, of course, but if there's any chance that I'd disturb him—"

"With the way this house is built, if you set off a cherry bomb in that room he probably wouldn't hear it next door. It's supposed to be a sitting room for the master suite, actually." Mrs. Ekberg pushed open an arched door and stood back for Molly to enter. "It was turned into a bedroom for Mr. Warren at the time of Mrs. Hudson's last illness, and he's never bothered to put it back as it was."

Molly wondered why the words sounded almost like a warning—until she stepped across the threshold.

Every room had an identity entirely its own, she'd always thought, a character that was built into the structure. It could be influenced by the furnishings and the decorating scheme, but not completely changed. Some rooms were feminine. Some were brisk, some relaxing, some peaceful.

This one, she thought, had a multiple-personality disorder.

The carpet was moss green, thick and plush. The hangings on the tall French doors that looked onto a tiny balcony and the gardens below were pale pink satin, elegantly draped. The small fireplace was topped with a white marble mantel. The chandelier was a dainty creation of Austrian crystal.

But the furniture that should have been scattered around the room—except for one gilt chair with a velvet-covered seat—was nowhere to be seen. Instead, at one side of the room was a hospital bed with a metal frame and not even a basic headboard—one of Meditronics' older models, Molly knew from her study of the company's catalogs. The blankets were tucked in neatly and the pillows plumped, but there was no bedspread and not even a night table.

Nearby was a tubular metal laundry rack, which had obviously served as a makeshift closet. There were still a couple of shirts hanging on it. A very masculine—and very worn—brown leather recliner stood in a corner next to a reading lamp.

In front of the windows, nearly blocking the view, was a huge old desk, its battered top almost as big as the bed. The gilt chair standing next to it looked as delicate in comparison as if it was built of toothpicks. Close by were the boxes Molly had brought that morning. *Watkins is even more efficient than I thought,* she concluded. He must have spirited them up the back stairs while she'd been talking to Luke.

"Every time I ask Mr. Warren if he doesn't want the room straightened out and that awful bed sent back to the attic," the housekeeper said, "he tells me just to leave it alone."

"Next time," Molly recommended, "don't ask."

Mrs. Ekberg smiled. "I'll keep that in mind. I'm sure it's not the kind of surroundings you're used to—"

"You can say that again. I've never had an office with a chandelier." Molly walked to the desk.

"I thought perhaps new draperies—"

"Heavens, no." She could almost hear what Luke would say if she started to redecorate.

Mrs. Ekberg looked disappointed. "But these are terribly faded."

"That doesn't mean it's my privilege to replace them."

"Very well, miss. If there's anything you want, just let Watkins or me know."

Molly lifted the lid off a box. "Some coffee in an hour?"

"And leave you alone till then?" There was an apologetic twinkle in the housekeeper's eyes. "Of course, miss. It's been a very long time, you see, since there's been a lady in the house. I've almost forgotten how to behave."

She left Molly shaking her head in confusion. There

hadn't been anything improper or impolite about Mrs. Ekberg's actions, but she'd sounded almost as if Molly was Oakwood's new mistress, not a temporary worker. *New draperies...anything you want...*

She shook her head at her own nonsense and went to work. Mrs. Ekberg had been friendly—that was all. The rest was entirely her imagination.

Warren appeared nearly an hour later, almost simultaneously with the coffee, wrapped in a dark red watered-silk dressing gown. The sheer splendor made Molly wonder how the same man who chose such an exotic fabric could ignore the confused state of the sitting room for years on end. But perhaps he hadn't bought the robe himself, she concluded. It looked like the sort of thing that might have been a Christmas gift.

He looked shamefaced. "I dropped off to sleep again after my breakfast," he admitted.

"Nothing wrong with that—but I'm awfully glad you're here now. Look at the letter I've just found. The handwriting alone is a treasure, but I don't have a hint what it means." She passed the pages across the desk and delighted in the sparkle that sprang to life in Warren's eyes. He looked better today, she thought. And though he'd leaned on the furniture as he crossed the room, he wasn't using the walker.

After lunch, Warren retired for another nap, and it was late afternoon before he reappeared. Molly had started a small pile of documents for his inspection, but instead of picking up the first one he looked at her and frowned. "Is it my imagination, or is it awfully quiet around here? And the dog's lying under my chair. Why isn't she out playing with your little girl?"

"Bailey? She's at the plant—in the day-care center."

"You took her all the way down there?"

"I had to pick up these boxes anyway."

"But now you'll have to drive across town to pick her up. That's ridiculous."

"Well, I can't bring her here."

Warren scowled. "Why not?"

"I hardly think she belongs at—"

"I insist."

Molly leaned back in her chair—neither the gilt and velvet one nor the recliner, but a small armchair she'd discovered downstairs. "Autocratic old soul, aren't you?" she said politely.

Warren smiled. "I figure there have to be some privileges to age and illness."

"Among them having your every request treated as a command?"

"That would be a good start, don't you think?"

"Why am I so certain that wasn't really a question?"

"Then you'll bring her?"

"I'll think about it." Molly glanced at her wristwatch. The timing, she thought, couldn't have been worse. She set a stapler atop the documents she was working on to serve as a paperweight and stood up. "I have to go and get her now, I'm afraid. The center closes in half an hour."

His brows drew together. "That proves my point. I'm feeling refreshed and ready to work, and you're leaving."

Molly waggled a finger at him. "You don't fight fair."

"Of course I don't. Now are you going to bring her? There are always at least three adults in this house, any one of whom is capable of keeping an eye on a small child."

"And I'm sure they'll be delighted to have baby-sitting added to their duties." She walked around the desk to stand beside Warren. "But it's sweet of you, it really is." Impulsively, she leaned over him and pressed a kiss on his forehead.

A voice from the doorway said, "There's your mommy."

Molly jerked upright so fast she almost lost her balance. She had no doubt, from the coolness in Luke's eyes, that he'd seen just enough to make him think the very worst. A minute earlier and he'd have seen the whole episode and known it for the innocent gesture it was. A minute later and he'd have seen nothing at all.

Her whole history with Luke, she thought irritably, seemed to come down to a matter of minutes.

Bailey came running, waving a sheet of blue construction paper. "Look what I made in day care, Mommy!"

She took the collage Bailey held out, but she looked from the child—who'd flung herself down beside the dog—to Luke instead. "Thank you for picking her up. But—"

He shrugged. "I was driving past the center on my way home, and it seemed a waste for you to have to go all the way back."

"It was very thoughtful of you," Molly said. "But the people at the center aren't supposed to let Bailey go with just anyone."

Warren made a sound that resembled a strangled sneeze.

Molly caught herself. "I mean—of course you're not just anyone, you're the boss. But still…"

"They're on the lookout for her father, I suppose you mean? Well, since it's pretty apparent I'm not him, the director didn't have any problem with me checking her out. And Bailey didn't, either. But if you do—"

Molly swallowed hard. "Of course not."

"Well, now," Warren said smoothly. "Since you don't have to make the trek down to the plant after all, Molly, let's settle down and get some work done. Lucas won't mind watching out for little Miss B, I'm sure. After all, he volunteered. Didn't you, my boy?"

Molly's jaw dropped. Luke was obviously speechless.

Warren sat back in his chair and smiled.

*   *   *

Molly tucked in fresh sheets on the bed in the Matthews's guest room while her printer spit out the last few pages of the chapter she'd finished that morning. She glanced over them and dropped the bundle into her briefcase. This afternoon—in just a few minutes—she'd take it to Oakwood for Warren to critique.

She leaned out the kitchen door and called to Bailey, who was lining up her agate collection on the deck railing, just as Megan's dark red BMW pulled into the driveway.

Molly's heart gave a jolt. She shooed Bailey off to wash her hands and went to meet her sister.

She hadn't seen Megan since the night of the dinner party, and their few phone conversations had been brief and light, mostly over details of the anniversary celebration, less than two weeks away. She'd let Megan set the pace in those conversations, and the subject of her pregnancy hadn't come up again. Molly had concluded, finally, that her sister had come to regret her impulsive outburst and was pretending the whole conversation had never happened.

Of course, it was Megan's choice. If she wanted to play her hand alone, that was her right. *You didn't like it when people tried to interfere and tell you what to do,* Molly reminded herself. And she definitely had no right to instruct her sister.

"Come on in," she said as Megan stepped onto the deck. "Mother's gone out to her card club, and I'll have to leave in a few minutes, but I think there's still some coffee."

"Oh—I forgot this was her club day." Megan tugged off her sunglasses and rubbed the bridge of her nose. "I didn't expect you to be here. I thought you were working down at Oakwood."

"That's where I'm headed. We've gotten into a sort of routine. Bailey's enrolled in the preschool down the street, so I work here till she gets home, and—"

But she wasn't thinking about the pattern of her days but about how pale Megan looked. In the week since the dinner party, she'd turned into a ghostly wraith with faint blue shadows under her eyes, despite the expert hand that had applied her makeup. To say nothing of the fact that she didn't seem to remember what day it was.

Megan sat at the kitchen table. "Do you like it? Oakwood, I mean?"

It was a throwaway question, Molly thought, asked more to keep the conversation going than because Megan really wanted to know. "Who wouldn't like it? I work here every morning, so Warren can be as lazy as he likes. Then we go to Oakwood in the afternoons." She glanced at the clock. "Bailey, it's time to get your things together. Are you going to take your dolls today, or the building blocks?"

"You take her with you?" Megan sounded incredulous.

Molly didn't blame her. "Warren insists. Just as he insists I come in time for lunch every day so we can talk over the progress we're making. I think he's just lonely, but—"

"So what do you do with the kid? I can't quite see her in that elegant dining room."

"You'd be surprised," Molly said dryly. "But usually she entertains the cook by playing with her food in the kitchen. Then she spends the rest of the time coloring, taking a nap, romping with the dog, fixing treats and exploring Oakwood—which the staff encourages her to regard as her private playhouse."

Megan shivered.

"I know—all those lovely breakable things. I walked into the drawing room one day last week and found her having a pretend tea party with Mrs. Ekberg—using the Haviland china. And when I nearly had a heart attack and asked Mrs. Ekberg not to let Bailey have quite so much freedom, she looked at me blankly and said that

the child was being very careful and she wasn't hurting
anything. And she *is* careful and she *hasn't* hurt anything, so…''

Megan didn't seem to be listening.

''But at least there haven't been any more tea parties.'' Molly asked bluntly, ''Meg, are you all right? I
mean—have you decided what to do about the baby?''

''What is there to do? Pregnancy's pretty much a one-
way ticket, wouldn't you say?''

Relief percolated through Molly's veins. ''Absolutely,
it is. But you don't have to take the flight alone.''

''I know. I just… I'm not ready to talk about it.''

Molly was sure that wasn't what Megan had started
to say.

''Actually, I'm glad to catch you,'' Megan went on
brightly. ''Would you ask Mrs. Ekberg if we can borrow
a dozen small tables and about fifty chairs from
Oakwood for Mother and Dad's anniversary party? I can
rent them, of course, but the ones at Oakwood are so
much nicer.''

''I'll ask today and let you know. Anything else I can
do? I feel like a dead weight where this party's concerned, you know—especially now that you're not feeling well.''

Megan shook her head. ''I think it's all under control,
and you have plenty to do, anyway. But I wondered…
Well, there's a Waterford crystal bowl I know Mother
would like as an anniversary gift. Should we go together
to buy it?''

''Depends on how pricey it is.''

''It's pretty high,'' Megan said frankly. ''But I didn't
mean we should go halves. I know you're on a tight
budget these days.''

*And you also know what it'll look like if Megan gives
crystal and Molly can only afford plain glass.…*

She didn't think Megan was acting out of snobbish-
ness, however, but genuine concern for her—so Molly

swallowed her pride. "Sure. It'd be great. But I'll pay my half—I just probably can't do it all at once."

Megan waved a hand. "Take your time. I'll go pick it up this afternoon."

Bailey came down the hall pushing a doll stroller piled with building blocks.

"That's quite the combination," Megan murmured.

Molly watched her sister's face and tried to decipher the emotions that played across it. Fear, she thought, was the principal one. "Being responsible for a child isn't as overwhelming as it looks," she said. "You and Rand will soon get used to it. When they put your own baby in your arms…" Megan didn't answer, but Molly saw the gleam of tears in her eyes, and she added quickly, "I'm sorry. I didn't mean to upset you."

Megan touched a tissue to her eyelids. "I know." She jumped up. "I've got to meet someone, and you need to get to work. Drop by tonight and take a look at the bowl if you like, before I wrap it. Rand's got some business thing, so it'll just be me." Her gaze came to rest on Bailey, waiting impatiently by the door. "Bailey can come, too, if she likes."

The invitation was surprisingly awkward from a woman of Megan's sophistication, but Molly was touched, for it was the first time Megan had indicated any real interest in the child.

She'll be all right, Molly told herself. *Megan will come around. And she'll be a good mom.*

By the time she filled her briefcase and touched up her lipstick, she was a good ten minutes behind Megan. But traffic was light for a change, and the day was perfect—so beautiful that if her car had been a convertible she'd have been tempted to put the top down. The move would be sheer foolishness, of course, since brilliant sunshine hardly corresponded with warmth. But she saw, as she stopped for a red light, that the drive-in ice cream shop on the corner was not only open, but there were a few cars around the building.

Bailey saw it, too. "I want ice cream," she announced.

"Another time. We're going to have lunch right now."

"But Luke's there."

Highly doubtful, Molly thought, until she noticed the black Jaguar tucked into a corner of the parking lot. There couldn't be many of those around Duluth. This one was half hidden by the building. *Bailey obviously doesn't need her vision tested,* she thought, *if she spotted that.*

Then she saw Luke. He was standing with his back to the street, but those broad shoulders and trim hips were unmistakable. As was the car he was standing next to—a dark red BMW with a woman behind the wheel.

I've got to meet someone, Megan had said. But... Luke?

And why shouldn't it be Luke? Molly asked herself. They'd been friends for years and years.

So why are they meeting at an obscure ice cream shop? asked a suspicious little voice in the back of her brain. *It's hardly Megan's sort of place.*

The light changed, and Molly drove almost automatically toward Oakwood. Was Megan turning to Luke for comfort and support? Why him and not her husband? Or was Luke the reason Megan was so plainly unhappy? Was it possible he was the father of the child Megan was carrying?

Molly felt sick.

Despite all the delays, she was still a few minutes early when she parked her car beside Oakwood and lifted out both Bailey and the stroller full of toys. "Let's walk in the garden for a minute before we go in," she said.

The crisp air cleared her head, and by the time she

turned toward the house Molly had regained her common sense.

Talk about making a mountain out of a molehill, she told herself. *Two people happen to meet at an ice cream shop in broad daylight, and you've turned it into a conspiracy!*

Warren made several suggestions which would improve the section of the book she was working on, and Molly listened carefully. His enthusiasm was so contagious that she didn't notice when he started to tire, and the sky was fading to dull gray before she realized that the zeal in his eyes was covering fatigue.

The instant she saw it, she stood up, cutting him off in the middle of a sentence. "Hold that thought," she said. "We'll start there tomorrow. But in the meantime, I'm not going to be responsible for you wearing yourself out."

"Trying to remember till tomorrow will be harder," Warren said, but she knew he was arguing more from habit than conviction, for the next minute he was trying to conceal a yawn.

She dropped a kiss on his forehead, as she had started to do every day when she said goodbye.

"Bring Miss B up to give me a hug before you go," he ordered.

"I will, unless she's asleep. Or you are."

"If it isn't nap time for one of us, it is for the other," Warren grumbled, and yawned again.

Molly was smiling as she ran down the stairs, briefcase in hand. There was no one in the drawing room—but she'd expected that. It was too late in the day for tea parties, even pretend ones.

Bailey was probably still in the kitchen. She'd helped bake cookies this afternoon, and she'd proudly carried a plate of them upstairs to her mother and Warren all by herself. A china plate, too. Molly thought Mrs. Ekberg needed her head examined to turn a three-year-old loose with anything so delicate.

The soft flicker of firelight from the library drew her close, and she paused by the door to peek in. Bailey had been known to snuggle up in one of the leather chairs by the fire as soon as it was lit and fall asleep waiting for Luke.

But tonight the chairs were empty. Luke was standing by the fireplace, however, with a glass in his hand. Was his brow creased with worry, Molly wondered, or was it only a trick of the firelight?

He'd been home a while, she noted, for he'd changed into jeans and a heavy pullover sweater that made his shoulders look even broader.

"Calling it a day, Molly?" he said. "Would you like a drink?"

She shook her head. "I told Megan I'd stop by tonight. She wanted to talk to me about something."

It was technically true—even if the something was a Waterford crystal bowl and not a baby. She watched him narrowly, wondering if he'd admit to having seen Megan. If she *had* confided in him...

"Have a good time," he said.

Which left her knowing precisely nothing. Of course, Molly hadn't really expected anything else.

The kitchen was warm and bright. The spicy fragrance of Bailey's cookies still hung in the air, mingling with the scents of wine and cream and herbs from the range, where the cook was stirring a sauce. "I thought you'd gone home an hour ago," she said cheerfully, and offered a spoon. "Would you taste this and see if it needs just a little more dill?"

Molly absently took the spoon. "Isn't Bailey here?"

"No. That's why I thought you'd gone home when she didn't come back after she took the cookies upstairs. You mean—"

"Then where is she?" Molly flung the spoon down and turned toward the hallway.

Mrs. Ekberg was in the dining room, shaking her head over a half-set table. "Miss Molly," she called. "Can you look at this tablecloth? I just don't think it's going to survive another laundering, and it's the only one left that fits the table when it's fully extended."

Molly hardly heard her. "Mrs. Ekberg, when was the last time you saw Bailey?"

"I don't remember. When she was taking your cookies upstairs, I suppose."

"But that was an hour ago!" Molly said frantically.

Mrs. Ekberg stared for an instant. "I'll check with Watkins," she said. Her voice was trembling. "She likes to help him polish silver. We had to give her a bath the other day, she was so covered with tarnish."

Luke appeared in the library door, glass still in hand, just as Mrs. Ekberg, looking grave, reappeared, with Watkins only half a step behind her.

"What's up?" Luke asked.

Molly tried, without success, to swallow the rock in her throat. Just speaking the fear out loud gave it more power, she thought. Made it more real. She had to force herself to say the words. "We can't seem to find Bailey."

CHAPTER SIX

THOUGH Molly's voice was little more than a whisper, the terror it held echoed through the hallway like a scream.

For one long instant Luke stared at her, and then he heard himself say, "She's three years old. What in the hell were you all thinking of to let her wander on her own?"

Watkins looked at his clenched hands. The cook flinched. Mrs. Ekberg seemed to shrink six inches.

Molly said, "Assigning blame isn't going to do any good now. It's my fault—I'm her mother, and it's my responsibility. Now do you suppose we could try finding her?"

"Sorry," Luke muttered. "Let's split up the house. She's got to be here somewhere."

"Probably curled up asleep in the most unlikely spot." But the quaver in Mrs. Ekberg's voice belied the comforting words.

They started to spread out through the lower floor. "Wait a minute," Molly said. "Does anybody know where the dog is?"

Because Bailey is apt to be nearby, Luke thought. "Probably with Dad." He was halfway up the stairs in two bounds.

Molly called, "Luke—wait a minute."

He looked over the railing at her. Her face was white, her eyes huge and dark. She looked very small and very fragile. "Warren must not find out that Bailey's missing."

"Then how do you expect me to—" But she was

right, he thought. The last thing his father needed was a shock. And the likelihood was that they'd find the child within minutes anyway, curled up with the dog in some out-of-the-way corner, and Warren would have been alarmed for nothing. "All right," he said, and went upstairs at a slightly slower pace.

When he tapped on the door of the master bedroom, there was no answer. Luke gently pushed the door open. Warren was stretched out on the velvet chaise longue in the bow window, eyes closed, his breathing steady.

The chaise had been Luke's mother's favorite resting place during her illness, looking out over the gardens she would never walk in again. He wondered if that was why Warren had adopted it.

Luke eased across the room, hoping the floor wouldn't creak. Lucky was nowhere in sight, but he thought she might be tucked away in the window nook behind the chaise.

Warren opened his eyes, but he didn't move. "What do you want, Lucas? Surely it's not time for dinner yet."

It was, as a matter of fact—but nobody was going to pay any attention to the time till Bailey was safe. Not that anyone would have an appetite anyway, except perhaps Warren.

"Not yet," Luke said. "There seems to be a problem in the kitchen that's holding things up."

"So why are you tiptoeing around my room?"

"Looking for Lucky."

Warren's eyebrows rose. "Feel the need for a good frolic, do you? Ask Miss B. She'll know."

I wish I could, Luke thought.

"She's a pretty little girl, isn't she?" Warren mused. He sat up and propped a pillow behind his back.

Please, Dad, Luke thought. *This is no time for a long chat.* If the dog wasn't here, then neither was Bailey, and he was frantic to get back to the search. But Molly's face flashed in his mind. Even in the midst of her pain, she'd been determined to protect Warren as long as possible—and if Luke walked out right now, the old man would know there was something going on. "She's cute, yeah."

"And as well-behaved as she is pretty, too. Don't you agree, Lucas?"

Oh, yes…except for this little matter of wandering off without permission.

Unless, of course, Luke thought, Bailey hadn't wandered off. His gut knotted. Now *there* was a thought that promised nightmares—and it came complete with a whole lineup of suspects. Bailey's father, snatching his daughter in violation of custody agreements. Some unknown monster who thought any kid who came from the Hudson mansion would be the ticket to a big ransom…

Somebody needs to sit by the phone. Just in case.

"Lucas?" Warren's voice had acquired a sardonic edge. "I didn't expect you to need a task-force study before you answered that question."

Luke blinked and tried to pull himself together. What was the question? Oh, right—*whether Bailey's well-behaved.* "She's amazingly good. And funny, too."

Warren nodded. "Molly's done a terrific job. She's had a tough time of it, you know. Being a single mom with all the pressures and responsibilities and almost no security… And she's got such a loving heart, too."

And right now her loving heart means I'm killing time here instead of searching. "Lovely woman."

"I've been thinking a lot about her lately, Lucas. About what's in the future for Molly and Bailey."

Luke felt as if he were standing off to the side of the room, watching himself carry on this conversation, so ridiculously lightweight in comparison to the reality downstairs. That distance added a sardonic note to his voice. "So what are you going to do? Propose, just to make it up to her?"

Warren's eyes closed for a moment, and when he

looked at his son again Luke saw a brilliance that startled him.

Warren said, "I'm so glad to know that you approve."

Now that was a smooth interpretation, Luke thought. One minute he'd been without a clue, the next his father had him practically walking Molly down the aisle. "I didn't say—"

"You used to tell us you wanted a sister," Warren murmured. "Though there is a bit of an age gap, of course."

Luke frowned. "Four years or so. That's—"

"Oh, no, I wasn't talking about Molly. She'd be your stepmother. I meant the age difference between you and Miss B. But that won't bother you, I'm sure—you play together so well."

I wouldn't mind anything he wants to do for Bailey, Luke thought. *Just as long as we can get her back here to enjoy it.*

He stood up, unable to stay still for another single instant. "Let me have a chance to think about all this, Dad."

Warren settled back on the chaise. "Don't take too long, my boy. I don't have all the time in the world, you know."

Luke felt as if he'd been gone forever, but Mrs. Ekberg was just coming out of the bedroom at the top of the stairs. She shook her head. "I've checked all the rooms up here. The attic door is locked, and—"

"Closets?"

"No sign of either Bailey or the dog. We could just call for Lucky, but Molly thought hearing that would upset Warren."

Damn Warren, Luke almost said. *He deserves a little upsetting—he's doing plenty of his own!*

Molly was standing at the library door. In her hands was a wad of bright pastel fabric. She looked at Luke, her face set and icy cold despite the fire's heat, and held the wad out to him. "It's her jacket. The cook found it in the kitchen."

Relief rocketed through him. "Then she's got to be somewhere in the house."

"Or else she's out there." She turned sightless eyes toward the glass panels beside the front door. "Without it."

With the wind picking up, and the temperature dropping. He had never felt so powerless in his life.

Luke reached for the telephone. "I'm calling the police."

Molly knew it was the next logical and necessary step. They needed help, and fast. But hearing Luke's voice as he summoned the authorities was like having her skin stripped away by inches.

My baby's gone, she thought helplessly.

Luke put the telephone down. "They'll have a car here in a few minutes. In the meantime, Watkins and I will start searching the grounds." His gaze flicked to Mrs. Ekberg and the cook. "You two, check right around the house. If she wandered outside—"

"She couldn't reach the doorbell," Molly said. "I had to lift her." She started for the door.

Luke caught her arm. "Somebody needs to stay by the phone."

His voice was gentle, but she heard the rough edge under it. He was afraid, she thought. Afraid of what they might find. And he didn't want her to be the one to stumble across—

She couldn't bear to think about it, and she cast her mind wildly for something else to hang onto. "I want Megan," she whispered. "I want my sister!" What she'd give right now to have that damned Waterford crystal bowl be her biggest problem...

"I'll call her," Luke said.

Megan must have had her hand on the phone, for in less than a minute he was back, easing Molly into a chair. "She's on her way." He crouched beside her, his gaze compelling her to look at him, to listen. "Perhaps you should call Bailey's father."

She shook her head.

"Molly, I really think—"

"No. And I'm not going to sit here beside a phone that isn't going to ring. I'm going out, right now, to look for her."

Luke bit his lip. "All right." He held her back from the door while he forced her arms into a thick, oversize wool jacket as if she were a child. He picked up a flannel-lined windbreaker for himself, and they went out together into the gathering dark.

Molly hadn't expected to need the coat. She'd pictured the scene so clearly in her mind, the moment she'd thought of the doorbell—Bailey wandering outside for some unknown reason, without her jacket because she didn't intend to stay out and play. Then the door blowing shut behind her. And, when she found she couldn't reach the bell, she wouldn't have thought of going round the house looking for a low window so she could get someone's attention. She was three, after all. She'd have sat down beside the front door, in the shelter of the juniper bush, to wait. And Molly would open the door and scoop her up—

She'd built the scene so well in her mind that she couldn't bring herself to believe, when she stood on the front steps, that there was no child huddled against the juniper bush. She stood absolutely still, staring at the place where she'd been so certain Bailey would be.

But there were all kinds of holes in the story she'd constructed. Unable to reach the bell, Bailey would have pounded on the door. And she'd have heard Luke's car come down the drive and run to meet him.

Molly gulped and braced herself and went into the

deep gray of evening. It wasn't as dark as she'd expected. Though in her mind time had stretched out like taffy, according to her watch barely twenty minutes had passed since she'd realized Bailey was gone.

But the shadows were almost worse than pitch blackness would have been, for they moved as the wind stirred the trees. And every movement made her heart jerk with hope, and then with disappointment.

The headlights of a car swept across the drive. Megan's BMW screeched to a halt in front of the house, and Molly ran toward it. Megan flung herself from the car, leaving the engine running and the door open, and swept Molly into her arms.

Molly let herself have the luxury of a fifteen-second-long hug. Megan kissed her cheek, patted her back and looked at Luke. "Mother and Dad are about two minutes behind me. I called them while I was driving down the hill. What else can I do?"

"Go sit with my father," he said promptly. "Whatever you do, don't tell him what's going on. Make some excuse for being here, and you might try to explain the screeching tires, too—"

Molly thought, *So he does know about Megan's condition. And he's assigning her a safe job.*

"And if the phone rings, grab it before he can."

"And still keep a lid on the story?" Megan said dryly. "Oh, that should be fun."

Another car pulled up behind the BMW, and Alix and Bernie got out. "My dear," Alix called. "This is horrible. How did it happen?"

"Doesn't matter, Mom," Megan said crisply. "Get your orders and save the explanations for later, okay?" She winked at Molly. "Keep your chin up. Bailey's a lucky kid. She'll be all right."

Lucky. For a moment, Molly had almost forgotten about the dog. The wind had risen, and it was hard to hear. Was that a dog's yelp, or a wild creature, or only her imagination?

As Molly's parents came up to them, Luke said, "I've been trying to convince Molly to call her ex-husband. I suppose he's got a right to know when Bailey's in danger—but we can also make sure he's where he's supposed to be and that he hasn't run off with her. But Molly doesn't—"

"He didn't snatch her," Molly said.

Luke stared at her. "And why, precisely, are you so certain of that?"

"Can't you take her word for it?" Alix asked.

"No."

"Then how about this?" Alix's voice dripped impatience. "We know he didn't do it because he's dead."

Luke drew back as if he'd been slapped.

Molly was too numb even to care. There were more important problems right now than trying to straighten out that complication.

Besides, Alix was absolutely correct, even if it was for all the wrong reasons.

Molly turned toward the side of Oakwood, where a narrow ravine edged between the trees. The woods were darker. In these conditions, she could walk within inches of Bailey and not see her.

Through the fogginess in her brain, she realized she'd come to accept the possibility that Bailey wasn't able to call for help.

Her parents took the strip between the front driveway and the street, and the staff moved around the far corner of the house. Luke, Molly noticed, stayed within yards of her, far enough away to search an additional strip of land, close enough that he could reach her in a few steps if...

She didn't want to think about that.

She thought instead about the pitifully slow progress they were making in covering the ground. "Strange," she said, "to send an able-bodied woman inside instead of putting her to work in the search."

Luke didn't look up from the leaf-strewn shadows he was inspecting. "Do you think you can cut out being jealous of your sister for one minute? You wanted her, she came, she's where she can do the most good right now. So lay off her, all right?"

Molly felt ashamed of herself, but not enough to admit it to him. "It's still odd."

"Would you rather I'd sent your mother up to soothe him? Look, you don't have to fuss about Megan being with Warren—it's clearly you he's got his eye on."

She thought she hadn't heard him right. "What?"

"You know, Molly, I intended for you to reawaken his interest in life in general, not in you specifically."

"I don't know what you mean."

"Oh, really? It hadn't occurred to you that he's planning wedding bells?"

She stood stock-still in the middle of a lighter patch of woods and stared at him. Suddenly it was all too much—the fear and the cold and the tension and the dread—and she started to laugh, bursts of giggles that quickly turned to sobs that shook her body like an aspen leaf.

In a moment, Luke was beside her, hands on her shoulders, shaking her. But the quaking only grew worse, and suddenly she couldn't get her breath.

Luke said something she didn't hear and dragged her against his body, and his mouth came down on hers, punishingly fierce.

Before she knew what she was doing, her hand had raised a red welt on his cheek, and her palm was stinging with the impact. "You just had to try it out, didn't you?"

Luke rubbed his cheek. "At least you're not hysterical any more. Now can we get down to business again?"

She was horrified to realize that for one instant Bailey

had been blanked out of her mind completely. She stumbled as she walked into the ravine that marked the edge
of Oakwood's grounds.

They had worked down the ravine quite a way when
the moon came out from behind a cloud, and she caught
the glint of its light against something high above her
head. "The treehouse," she said. "She was fascinated
by the treehouse."

Luke shook his head. "I haven't been up there
since..."

Since the night before his mother died. *Don't kid
yourself, Molly—it's not you he's thinking about.*

He didn't finish. "Besides, it's locked up tight."

"To keep kids out. But Bailey wouldn't know that."

Molly waited at the base of the tree while he climbed,
and when he shouted that there was no sign, she sagged
against the rough bark and folded her arms across her
chest as if to hug the child who wasn't there.

Bailey, you can't just have vanished. Where are you?

Luke was climbing down. She closed her eyes and
listened to the rhythmic scrape of his shoes against the
treehouse ladder. But between those sounds, there was
something else, only once—a faint far-off cry that might
have been the yelp of a dog.

Luke leaped the last two steps and stood dusting off
his hands. "I think—"

"Listen!"

Luke tipped his head. The wind calmed, and they both
heard. "Down by the lake," he said.

For a moment, they stared at each other, silently ac-
knowledging what neither had dared to say before—that
the lake was a last resort. If Bailey had fallen into that
inland sea, the largest freshwater lake in the world, the
graveyard of thousand-foot-long ships whose wreckage
had yet to be located, she might never be found. So they
had looked everywhere else first. Now there was only
the lake left.

And if they found Lucky pacing the seawall, looking across the water in search of her small companion...

I might just throw myself in, too, Molly thought.

She jogged from time to time, but she was in no shape for this race. Her lungs were shrieking for relief when, a couple of yards behind Luke, she reached the concrete wall that protected the shore from the pounding waves.

And saw nothing but Luke poised atop the seawall, silhouetted against the moonlit water, and the six-foot drop beyond him to where waves sloshed over the rocky lake bottom and shattered in white foam against the concrete barricade.

Then the dog barked from out of nowhere. It seemed to Molly that Luke leaped off the wall into empty air, and she reached out to stop him an instant too late. Had his feet slipped on the wet concrete? Or had he really jumped?

She crept closer, cautious of her balance, and saw him, waves breaking around his knees as he sloshed toward a dark, wet lump huddled against the seawall twenty feet down the shore. She strained to see and recognized Lucky leaning against the concrete with her feet in the water, her claws scrabbling on the rocky bottom. And pressed between the dog's body and the wall, just above the water, was a sopping, bedraggled bundle.

"Good dog," Luke said, and reached over Lucky to drag Bailey into his arms.

Molly scrambled along the wall till she was directly above them and waited an eternity until he boosted his burden to her. "She's breathing," he said.

Bailey whimpered, "I want Mommy."

Hot tears streamed down Molly's face. "Mommy's here, love. Luke, she's so cold!"

"Of course she's cold. She's soaked. Get her clothes off."

Had he lost his mind? "What do you mean, *off?*" She stared at him in horror, then remembered his medical training and began to fumble with Bailey's dripping sweatshirt.

"I mean, strip her." He heaved the dog out of the water and pulled himself onto the wall. "The wind hitting her wet clothes is sucking the heat straight out of her body." He tore off his windbreaker, pulled his sweater over his head and put the jacket on.

Molly fought to get Bailey out of her sodden jeans. The moment the child was free, she reached for his sweater, but Luke scooped Bailey against his bare chest, draped his sweater across her back like a blanket and folded the windbreaker around both of them. "Body heat," he said. "Hurry."

"Mommy," Bailey said. It was a hopeless, helpless little murmur that nearly broke Molly's heart.

She didn't know how she managed to stay even with Luke's longer stride, even burdened as he was. Lucky bounded toward the house ahead of them, barking wildly.

"Too bad she couldn't do that before," Luke said. "But she was using all her strength to keep them both from going into the drink."

A siren shut off abruptly in the driveway as they came around the corner of the house. Why had it taken so long for the police to arrive, Molly wondered. Or was her mind fooling her again? Had they been out searching for only a few minutes, even though it felt like years?

Luke waved down a patrolman, and within a minute they were in a police car, headed for the hospital. Bailey was still snuggled close against Luke's body, and Molly was using the sleeve of her wool jacket to dry the child's straggly hair.

"My badge," Bailey murmured. "I want...badge."

Molly thought that weak little voice was the most beautiful sound in the world. "Later, honey. We'll get it for you later."

* * *

The emergency room crew shut the door of the treatment room in Molly's face. Very politely, of course, and with the best of explanations. She'd be in the way while they got Bailey stabilized and warm once more. And then she'd need X rays, to make sure she hadn't gotten water in her lungs. But after that... Just as soon as Molly could be with her daughter, they'd come and get her.

Luke coaxed her to a quiet corner of the waiting room, but Molly couldn't sit still. "She'll be okay, won't she?"

"Sure," he said. Then, as if he recognized how very unconvincing he'd sounded, he went on. "She was conscious when I pulled her out—that's a good sign. The dog's body broke the force of the waves and the wind, and because they were huddled together they didn't lose heat quite as quickly."

She looked at him, drew a deep, shaky breath and relaxed a tiny bit. "What about Lucky?"

"She looked all right. Maybe some frostbite on her paws. I don't know. Depends on how long they were in the water, I suppose. Watkins will make sure the dog's taken care of."

"I hope he makes sure she gets a couple of steaks. No, I don't—I want to do that myself, and feed them to her bite by bite." She tried to wipe the tears away.

"Molly." He was staring at his shoes and the puddle of lake water that had dripped from his jeans, and his voice was heavy. "That first day you brought her to Oakwood, I told Bailey I'd take her down to the lake. And I didn't do it. I never got around to it—"

"And you think that's why she went, so you're blaming yourself? Don't, Luke."

"You don't hold it against me?"

Molly shook her head. "I could just as easily blame my father. He's the one who taught her to love the lake. It's not your fault, Luke, any more than it's his."

He looked at her for a long moment. "Thanks,

Molly.'' He reached out to her, and his hand closed slowly around hers. Molly looked at their linked fingers, his tanned, hers much paler.

She had cared about him once—as a girl cares. And she knew he'd been right, all those years ago, that what she felt was far closer to infatuation than to love. When she had first come back to Duluth, she'd thought she was indifferent to him. She'd intended to do her job, live her life and pay no heed to Lucas Hudson.

But now... Now she felt confused.

She'd seen him in a different light tonight, that was certain. She'd known that Bailey thought he was pretty neat, for Bailey had told her. But Luke had been harder to read until tonight. He'd been stunned by the child's disappearance and determined to find her at any cost to himself—traits that would win him a place in any mother's heart.

She had to admit that she still got a lump in her throat whenever she closed her eyes and pictured the way he'd flung himself off the seawall, heedless of anything except the need to get Bailey out of the lake.

Bailey. That, of course, was the common thread. He'd fallen in love with her little girl—which wasn't much of a surprise. That sparkling child could walk off with almost anybody's heart—and it was clear she'd added Luke's to her collection.

What in the hell were you thinking of to let her wander on her own? he'd said in that first stunned moment when Molly had told him Bailey was gone. And he'd kissed her tonight not out of any fondness—she could never forget the bruising force of that kiss—but to shock her out of hysteria and back to the business of finding Bailey.

Even when he hadn't been a hundred percent focused on the child, he'd had nothing flattering to say to Molly. *Do you think you can cut out being jealous of your sister for one minute?* he'd asked. And that crack he'd made about Warren asking her to marry him... Luke obviously hadn't any personal feelings on the matter, except that he'd clearly thought his father had lost his mind.

Bailey was a different matter. It was Bailey who kept him sitting here, even though he was dripping and chilled, waiting to be certain she was all right. It was Bailey who occupied his mind. Bailey...

Ever so slowly, she pulled her hand away from his. Or had he purposely loosened his hold and let her slip away?

Luke sat up a little straighter. "So," he said. He was trying very hard, she thought, to sound completely normal. "As long as we've got time to kill, why don't you tell me how you got the bruise? If it wasn't the ex, who punched you in the face? And why wouldn't you tell me what happened?"

"You expected me to explain?" Molly countered. "It was a job interview. Questions about personal business have no place in—"

Luke snorted. "I suppose you're going to file sexual harassment charges for the way I treated your hysteria tonight?"

"Of course not. Assault would be more like it."

"That's a relief. And by the way, you haven't answered the question this time, either. Who punched you?"

A nurse—not the one who'd asked Molly to wait outside —came into the waiting room. "Are you Bailey's parents? You can come in now."

Molly watched the shadow settle across Luke's face, and the heaviness that had lain across her heart for more years than she wanted to remember translated itself into a new and different sort of pain.

She stood up and very deliberately stretched out her hand to him.

A trace of a frown flickered across his face. Then he

folded his fingers around hers and walked beside her to a cubicle.

Just outside the half-closed door, a young man was scribbling on a chart. He looked up and said, "That's one fortunate kid, you know. We want to keep an eye on her for another few hours—keep a warm IV running, that sort of thing. But if she doesn't have any further problems you'll be able to take her home yet tonight."

Molly didn't realize till then she'd been holding her breath.

Perched high atop a hospital bed, propped with a stack of pillows, Bailey sat with a tray table arranged across her lap and a mug in her tiny hands. She looked like a doll among the multitude of blankets folded around her.

The moment she saw Molly, Bailey held out her arm to display the IV drip. "Mommy, they stuck a *needle* in me." She was obviously incensed. "And it's *still there*."

Luke chuckled. "You go right ahead and complain, princess."

She turned her big brown eyes to him. "Will you make them take it out, Luke?"

"Later. They're pretty busy right now, so we'll have to wait our turn again." He laid a hand on her shoulder.

Was it only her imagination, Molly wondered, or were his fingers trembling? She moved to the other side of the bed and leaned on the railing. "What are you drinking, Bailey?"

"Hot chocolate." The child looked a little guilty. "I forgot about having to ask you first."

"It's all right. I'm sure the doctor knows what he's doing." Molly pushed a lock of dark hair from the child's forehead. Her hair was dry but it felt sticky from the lake water.

Bailey pushed the cup away. "Did you bring my badge?"

Molly had almost forgotten. "No, honey. But it'll be

waiting for us. Was it in your pocket?'' She'd left the sodden clothes on the seawall, but there'd be plenty of time to get them later.

Bailey shook her head. ''It went down in the lake. It blew away and went out in the water, so I climbed down off the wall like I do off the jungle gym at the park. It wasn't very far.''

Molly's heart was quaking. A six-foot wall, and Bailey had simply hung by her hands and dropped off it?

''But I couldn't reach it. And the wall was too slick so I couldn't climb back up, and Lucky jumped down and splashed me and got me all wet. And then I got cold.'' She yawned.

''But now you're warm again.'' Molly tried to smile.

''The badge,'' Luke said. ''The damned badge. I'm sorry, Molly. You didn't want her to have it in the first place.''

''Put a plug in it, Luke, will you? No one could have anticipated that she'd go in the lake...'' Molly couldn't keep her voice from shaking.

Luke reached across the bed to squeeze her hand.

Bailey's second yawn was even bigger, and she let her head drop on the pillow. ''I still like the lake, even if it was all wet and nasty.''

They stood there till she was asleep. ''That's good,'' Luke said. ''That she still likes the lake, I mean. She could have been so traumatized that she'd never go near water again.''

Molly nodded and let her head sink down to rest on the chrome rail of Bailey's bed.

''You're exhausted,'' Luke said.

''I'm not leaving.''

''Of course not. But surely I can find you a chair.'' But he didn't step away from the bed. ''Molly,'' he said quietly. ''I know you probably didn't even hear what the nurse was saying out there—about parents, plural. But thanks for letting me come in. For letting them think I'm her father.''

She looked at him, and at their clasped hands, and then at the face of her sleeping daughter. ''Why not?'' she said. ''After all…it's true.''

CHAPTER SEVEN

FROM out in the hallway Molly could hear the clinking of stainless steel instruments as a cart was wheeled by. Above her head, one of the fluorescent lights hummed in a off-key pitch that grated on her nerves. But there was no other sound.

She watched her daughter's face and stroked the child's hair. Her fingertips, she noted with detached interest, weren't shaking at all. That was just as well, for now that she'd made her declaration it was too late to worry.

But she couldn't deny that the longer the silence lasted the more apprehension oozed through her veins until finally she could bear it no longer. Slowly, she raised her head until her gaze met Luke's.

If she'd suddenly sprouted horns, he couldn't have looked more flabbergasted. Almost dazed, she thought. As if he was staring straight through her.

Then, as she watched, his gaze focused on her face. "You've snapped," he said firmly. "It's been a terrible few hours, and now that the stress is finally off—"

Of course, she hadn't really expected anything else. Nevertheless, Molly's shoulders drooped as the weight of fatigue settled onto them once more. But this exhaustion wasn't from the evening's strain. it was a tiredness born years ago. "Fine," she said. "I've snapped. Call the men in the little white coats."

"You're not..." He paused. "You haven't mistaken me for someone else?"

"Like who? Santa Claus? Come off it, Luke. I'm not having hallucinations."

He relaxed. She watched the taut muscles of his face ease. "Well, in that case... This is actually pretty funny, Molly. Haven't you overlooked one minor detail?"

"You mean the fact that we never quite made love?"

"Well, it does seem—"

"The key word, of course, is *quite*. Remember, Luke? You said yourself that another minute and it would have been too late. Well, it *was* too late. Making love is a process—and even though we didn't finish, we'd certainly started."

"That's impossible."

"It wouldn't be the first time it's happened—two kids fooling around, never quite going the whole way but getting plenty excited. I actually thought once of going on the speaking circuit—talking to teenagers as a living example of why keeping all their clothes on and both feet on the floor is such a good idea. Showing them the impossible baby." Molly knew she sounded bitter, and she was afraid he'd misunderstand the source of that feeling. "Bailey's a blessing, the best thing that ever happened to me. But coming to terms with how it happened was a different matter altogether."

Luke shook his head.

She had known, of course, that he wasn't likely to believe her. She'd had enough trouble in the beginning accepting it herself. But seeing his doubt, feeling the waves of disbelief, infuriated her. "If you want blood tests, Luke, we're all right here in the hospital—and they already have plenty of Bailey's, no doubt."

He seemed not to have heard her. "What about your husband?"

Molly sighed. "There never was one. Mother couldn't bear the idea of me having a baby without a wedding ring, so when I was in Chicago she kept up the fiction of a marriage, and after a while a divorce. Then when I came home and her friends started wondering rather loudly why Bailey's father didn't help support her—as if it was any of their business—she killed him off.''

"And you played along with it."

"I didn't even know she'd manufactured a story till I got home. And then what was I supposed to do about it? Announce to the world that my mother had created the whole scenario in order to save face with her friends? Call her a liar while my daughter and I are living in her house, eating her food, wearing clothes she laundered? Besides, that's hardly the point just now, is it?''

"No," he agreed. "It's the other incredible story that's the problem.''

Molly faced him squarely. "Suit yourself." Her voice was almost lifeless. "Forget it. I never said a word, all right?''

"Molly—"

"Now just go away," she said, "and leave me and *my* daughter alone.''

Once, when he'd been just a kid and learning to ride, Luke had been kicked squarely in the stomach by a horse. It was the only time in his life he'd felt anything like the blow Molly had dealt him tonight.

She looked like an angry Madonna as she bent over the hospital bed, tucking the blankets closer around...

His daughter?

No, he told himself. It was completely, absolutely impossible. For some incomprehensible reason, she'd decided to try out an incredible scam.

As he walked down the long hallway toward the emergency room exit, he stumbled over nothing but air. An aide coming toward him gave him a suspicious look. *She probably thinks I'm intoxicated,* Luke thought. *And she's right—only the poison in my system is accusations, not alcohol.*

He walked unseeing through the waiting room, and he was at the door when a woman approached. He turned away, unwilling to attempt to be polite to a stranger wanting the time, much less a staff member wanting information.

"Luke!" Megan Bannister grabbed his arm. "You look awful. Is she... Has she—?"

He shook his head to clear it. "Bailey's fine. She's asleep, and Molly's with her."

Megan's face had gone ashen, and she swayed. Quickly, Luke guided her to the nearest chair. "Put your head down," he ordered.

"I'm not going to faint. I just thought for a moment..." She shuddered. "If I had to go tell my parents that their granddaughter was gone..."

Luke put his arm around her. "Don't torment yourself, Meg. She's all right. She can probably go home in a few hours."

She turned her face against his shoulder. "Oh, Luke, what would I do without you?"

"A better question is what you're doing here when you should be home with your feet up."

Megan shook her head. "If I hadn't come, Mother would have—and I think Molly would much rather have me. That's not saying a whole lot, as I'm sure my little sister can function quite well without me. But after some of the run-ins they've had over—" She stopped awkwardly, and her color came back in a embarrassed flood.

"Over the late and not lamented ex-husband?"

Megan wouldn't look at him. "That's part of it. Look, I don't know what happened to my presence of mind, but I shouldn't have said—"

"Why not? Friends tell friends what they need to know."

"And you need to know about Molly's ex?"

He nodded. He felt almost as if he was going behind Molly's back to ask. But that was stupid. He had every right in the world to check out her story in any way he could. "And Bailey's father." The words tasted funny on his tongue.

Megan laughed. "You sound as if they were two different people."

"Weren't they?" There was no amusement in his voice.

She bit her lip. "Okay, Luke—I'll tell you what I know. But it isn't much, all right? So don't expect the encyclopedia. There never was a husband. And Molly would never tell anyone who Bailey's father was."

Molly would never tell. That wasn't the same as saying Megan didn't know. "You must have an idea."

"How? I went away to college, Molly stayed here. And we never did confide much in each other. We certainly didn't share insights on our men of the moment. She could have been dating every man at the university."

"Or somebody else altogether."

Megan nodded. "All I know is, she was fighting morning sickness at my wedding."

The wedding had been at Christmastime, Luke remembered. He'd been an usher, Molly the maid of honor. She'd been very pale that day in her dark green velvet gown, and just a little shaky. The guests had probably thought it was nerves. Luke had assumed—a bit vainly, perhaps—it was because she was seeing him for the first time since he'd given her the lecture of her life.

But if she'd been ill at Megan's wedding...

"She didn't tell anyone," Megan went on. "In fact, she waited till after my honeymoon was over, and then she called a family meeting and announced that she was expecting a baby."

"I bet that went over well," Luke said dryly.

Megan rolled her eyes. "Mother exploded and demanded a name...and Molly refused. I've never seen anyone with so much dignity. Little Molly—who would have believed it?"

I would, he thought. *Because she displayed it for me, too.*

"It was like she was sealed inside a plastic cube," Megan said, "where nothing could reach her. I don't think she'd have talked under torture because—let's face it—my mother tried. So Molly went off to Chicago to finish school and make a life for herself and her baby. The whole thing makes my problems look kind of small, doesn't it?"

Luke gave her a hug. "Feeling any better?"

"No. But I've resigned myself. There's no reason my baby shouldn't be all right, and that's the important thing."

"You're important, too," he reminded.

She smiled at that, but he didn't think she really believed it. "Where's Bailey's room? Which way do I go?"

"How about home?"

Megan shook her head. "You all got here without a car, and if Bailey's released how are you going to get her home?"

"Taxis are a wonderful invention." But he relented and gave her the room number. "I'll see you tomorrow, probably."

"You're leaving? Oh, of course—you're still squishing around in wet shoes yourself."

He waited till Megan was out of sight down the long hall before he called a cab, and he went into the bracing cold of the evening to wait, hardly feeling the wind against his damp jeans.

A chilly evening. It had been cold that October night in the treehouse, too. He'd been miserable, shattered at the news that his mother, who two weeks before had seemed perfectly healthy, had—at most—days to live. He didn't remember climbing the tree. He'd automatically fled to the security of his childhood. And he'd sat

there in the dark and cold, feeling the finality of the
darkness and coldness that was creeping over his mother.

That was when Molly had appeared.

She hadn't asked his permission to join him. She'd
seemed to know he'd tell her to go away. She'd let herself into the treehouse, turned on the electric heater and
sat beside him on the bunk. Without a word she reached
for his hands and held them between hers, rubbing
gently till the chill was gone.

And then she'd talked—not in the platitudes so many
others had tried to feed him, but with gentle understanding. And she'd listened while he poured out his feelings,
spilled fears that were so deeply entrenched he'd been
almost incoherent. And yet she had understood.

He'd been spent, finally, and relaxed for the first time
in days, and he'd turned to her in silent gratitude.

But she was as generous in her kisses as she'd been
in her compassionate silence, and he hadn't wanted to
stop. Neither had she. There was no question in his mind
that Molly wanted him as much as he wanted her. And
so they'd lain together on the bunk and explored each
other and taken comfort in their closeness…

We didn't finish, Molly had said, *but we'd certainly
started.*

She was right. He'd told her once that another minute
and he wouldn't have been able to send her away. But
it would be more accurate to say that it had been a matter
of seconds.

At the last possible moment, his mother's face had
flashed before him. He saw her eyes, racked with pain
not only from her illness but from his conduct. He was
disgusted with himself, and in his guilt he'd lashed out
at Molly.

His mother was dying. And here he was…

He didn't realize he'd said it aloud until the crudeness
of the words had sent ugly color flaring into Molly's
face. But even then she hadn't struck back. She'd looked

at him levelly, and then she'd slid off the bunk and reached for her clothes, and before he'd found his voice she'd dressed and left.

His mother had died the next day. After the funeral services, when the Hudsons' friends, relatives and employees gathered at Oakwood, Molly had been among them, standing with her parents, holding an untouched cup of punch. He'd managed to get her alone without drawing anyone's attention in the small sun room at the back of the house.

He'd intended to apologize both for his words and for his conduct. But she didn't seem to hear anything he said. She looked at him like a zombie—what was the comparison Megan had made tonight? *Like she was sealed inside a plastic cube.*

He'd been afraid for her. Unintentionally, he had taken advantage of her warmth, her inexperience, her willingness. She didn't seem to understand the danger she'd put herself in—or that another man might not hesitate to use her. She didn't seem to see that her innocence invited that very sort of man.

She'd let him talk, and then she'd said, "I only wanted you to feel better."

Luke had exploded. "That's exactly what I'm talking about! And you can stop looking at me like that. It isn't going to happen again—not ever. And for heaven's sake don't be stupid enough to take up with some jerk just because you're trying to prove something to me."

She had said, "I love you, Luke. I'll always love you."

"You aren't old enough to know what love is," he'd snapped. "You're only infatuated, and you'd better get over it." And in frustration, Luke had turned away. He'd done all he could. If she was naive enough to get herself involved in something worse, it wasn't his fault.

But he'd been wrong about what she might do. She hadn't bounced straight to another man—there hadn't been time. If she'd been suffering from morning sickness at Megan's wedding, just two months later...

"Hey, buddy," the taxi driver called. "You the one that wants a ride? 'Cause I'm leaving one way or the other."

Luke directed the cabby to stop in front of Oakwood, paid his fare and walked slowly down the drive. But instead of the long rows of pine trees, he was seeing the wide aisle of the church where Megan and Rand had been married. Megan, excited and happy in her white satin with the marabou trim and the huge bouquet of white roses.

And Molly, paler than ever against the forest green of her dress, clutching the dark fur muff that she carried instead of flowers. Pale, he'd thought, because she had to face him for the first time since he'd made it clear her infatuation wasn't going to lead anywhere.

But it had led somewhere—and Molly had known it. She'd known when she walked down that aisle in her dark green velvet, no doubt praying that she wouldn't be sick in public, that she was carrying his child.

And she hadn't told him. Not till tonight, when he'd almost lost the daughter he'd never known he had.

He'd expected that after their painful confrontation she'd try to get even with him for rejecting her. He'd just hoped she wouldn't hurt herself in the process. She hadn't done what he'd anticipated—but she'd gotten even, all right.

She had deliberately cheated him of his daughter.

For a long time after he walked out, Molly stood very still beside Bailey's bed, elbows propped on the railing, face in her hands.

What had she expected, anyway? That he'd throw his arms around her in delight at the news that he'd suddenly acquired a daughter? Rush straight out and buy cigars?

Run through the hospital corridors shouting, "It's a girl!"?

You just blasted the man's whole life, she told herself. Or at least, that was what she'd done if he believed her. And if he didn't believe her... Well, she'd decided long ago that self-pity was a waste of time.

If Luke wanted to pursue the blood tests she'd mentioned, of course she'd cooperate. She could understand if he needed to be certain. It *was* a quaint little story, after all.

As a matter of fact, in order to prove she was telling the truth, she could demand that he go through with the tests. But she wouldn't force the issue. Under the circumstances, being dubious—feeling doubts—was a sensible sort of reaction. But to flatly deny the possibility...

A man who had to be coerced even to admit that he might have fathered a child wasn't much of a father. Bailey deserved better than that. In fact, having no father at all would be worlds better than having a reluctant one.

You should have kept your mouth shut, Molly told herself.

Two scalding tears rolled down her cheeks just as a tap sounded on the door, and she turned away to wipe her face.

"Hi," Megan said. "I ran into Luke in the lobby, and he filled me in."

Luke had filled her in? In the frame of mind he'd been in, he might have said anything. Just short of panic, Molly faced her sister. But there seemed to be nothing in Megan's expression except concern for Molly and tenderness when she moved to the side of the bed and looked at Bailey.

Molly breathed a little easier.

"So I stopped to phone Mother and Dad with a report before I came on back here. I hope you don't mind me interfering?"

Molly shook her head. "Of course not. I hadn't even

thought about calling. I wonder if anyone's talked to Warren?''

"I broke the news to him as gently as I could after you found her, and Mrs. Ekberg was sitting with him when I left. Besides, Luke's going straight home, isn't he? He'll take care of the rest, I'm sure."

Molly wouldn't bet any money on Luke's destination. And she wondered, even if he did go to Oakwood, exactly what he would tell his father. Part of her would love to be a mouse in that corner. The rest of her shuddered away from the very idea.

"You haven't actually been here that long, anyway," Megan pointed out. "Even though I'll bet it feels like all night."

No, Molly thought. *It feels more like a whole lifetime.*

"So give me all the details. Remember, I was stuck on the sidelines with Warren while all the excitement was going on. I couldn't even shout downstairs for an update."

Briefly, Molly told her. Her voice shook when she relived the brief space between Luke's leap off the sea-wall and the moment she once more had her baby—frighteningly cold, but breathing and conscious enough to want her mother—in her arms.

"Luke was quite the hero tonight, wasn't he?" Megan said. Her tone was careless, but Molly knew better than to take it at face value.

"Straight out of legend," she said dryly. "Silver armor and all."

Bailey stirred, and Megan looked at her. "I got the notion—foolish, I suppose—that he's thinking of trying out for a new role." She glanced at Molly. "As Bailey's stepfather."

She sounded amused, Molly thought, and bewilderment tugged at her. Megan didn't know the truth, that was plain, for her comment would have been deliberately cruel, and that wasn't like Megan. So was she using humor as a shield to feel out an unwelcome suspicion that Luke might be developing an interest in someone else? Or was she being absolutely straightforward? Totally wrong, of course—but with good intentions nonetheless?

Molly decided that a comment as ambiguous as that deserved a painfully direct question in return. "Do you object?"

"Me?" Megan's eyebrows arched. "Of course not. Go for it, darling."

Too late, Molly realized that she'd snared herself in the trap she'd set for Megan. "No," she said hastily. "That's not at all what I meant. He's not...and I wouldn't... It's just that..." She stammered to a halt; she could hardly say, *I only wanted to know if you're having an affair with him.*

Megan's smile was tolerant. "Of course," she said gently. "I'll forget the whole thing, I promise, now that you've assured me there's nothing to it. Oh, did I mention that Mother wants to talk to you? I told her you were pretty busy at the moment and you'd probably just wait till you got home."

Molly managed a smile. "Thanks, Meg."

"No trouble at all. I'll accept applause later for my role in keeping her away from the hospital." Megan reached across the narrow bed to touch Molly's arm. "Mother means well, you know."

"If you tell me she's just eager to help, I will bite you."

Megan frowned. "I'm not defending her, you understand, just explaining. But I'm surprised I have to, Molly. With the way she was raised, of course she does whatever she has to in order to save face, to appear as good as the rest of the crowd. She was tormented by other kids all through her childhood, you know, because she didn't fit in. She didn't speak properly because her parents didn't know how, and her clothes weren't just out of fashion, they were patched and faded and all the wrong size. She didn't own a winter coat till she went to work and earned it.''

Molly's eyes were wide.

''She scrabbled herself up from something so far below poverty there isn't even a word to describe it. She remade herself. Did you know her name was Alice originally? But the abuse of those early years left scars. She can't stand the thought that someone might be pointing at her, criticizing her, making fun of her—because she lived with cruelty for too many years to forget it. I thought surely you'd understand how inadequate she feels, Molly. You're the brains in this outfit, not me.''

''She's never told me any of that! I think you're wrong that I'm the brains—but you're certainly the favorite.''

Megan shrugged. ''If so, it's because I went along. I was a good girl. I complied. And I fulfilled her dreams—acquiring the wealthy husband, the blue-blooded relatives, the perfect house. And becoming the social leader that even the social leaders look up to.'' Her voice was full of irony.

''I knew those things were important to her,'' Molly said softly. ''I didn't know why. No wonder, when I announced that I was pregnant and there was no chance I'd marry the father of my baby, she went up in smoke.''

''And she told a whole lot of very silly stories that I'm sure she regrets. But now, of course, to admit what she's done would set off the old cycle again, make her the focus of criticism and gossip. So she's stuck between wanting to preserve her image and wanting to make everything right with you again.'' Her gaze rested thoughtfully on Bailey. ''She doesn't know how to bridge that gap, Molly. She's afraid to get too attached to either of you. Afraid you'll leave again.''

''She seems to be doing her best to drive me away.''

Molly shook her head. "Between the advice and the criticism—"

"Probably that's exactly what she's doing. Not on purpose, of course." Megan hesitated, then said more softly, "I think I can understand how she feels, Molly. I had time to think tonight, too, when Bailey was missing. I realized what I was giving up by not getting to know her." There was pain in her voice. "And I faced up to why I've been so distant and so rude."

Molly held her breath, afraid that the slightest sound would break the mood.

"I was jealous of you because you had what I wanted—a healthy baby. And I didn't want to get close to Bailey because it hurts too much to be reminded of the child I lost."

Molly's chest felt like a boa constrictor had seized her. "I didn't know. I'm sorry, Meg. There's so much I didn't know."

"Don't blame yourself. No one knew at the time. I miscarried so early in the pregnancy that we hadn't even told Mother and Dad about the baby."

Molly remembered something her father had said about Megan not wanting to have children. It would have been a horribly insensitive remark if he knew what had happened. So obviously he didn't know.

But it was equally apparent that Luke did. No wonder he'd sent Megan upstairs to sit with Warren instead of out in the cold to search! He'd wanted to protect her in this second possibly delicate pregnancy.

And no wonder Megan had been of two minds about being pregnant—pleased about the baby, frightened of the possibility of another miscarriage.

"And then, afterward, Rand didn't want to tell anybody what had happened," Megan went on. "He said they'd just ask nosy questions and offer awkward sympathy. And there'd soon be another pregnancy, anyway,

so there was no sense in talking about the one that had
gone wrong."

Molly had her own opinions about that, but she decided it would be prudent to keep them to herself just
now.

"Only there wasn't. It's been more than two years."

"But you have another chance," Molly said. "And
this time will be different. Lots of women miscarry for
all sorts of reasons. It doesn't mean you will again."

She would do anything in her power to be able to
wipe the haunted look from Megan's eyes. But Molly
knew only one thing would accomplish that—holding
her baby in her arms.

And Megan would have the additional joy of having
a loving husband, a happy father, at her side in that
moment.

Bailey stirred and opened her eyes and cried out, confused by the unfamiliar surroundings, and Molly
scooped her up.

It's you and me, honey, she thought as she held her
daughter. *That's all there's going to be. And that's all
we need.*

When her head finally touched her own pillow, Molly
dropped like a rock into sleep. She woke knowing it was
late and heard Bailey's cheerful chatter coming from the
kitchen. She wrapped herself in a bathrobe and followed
the sound.

Bailey was daintily nibbling a doughnut and in the
process showering powdered sugar over table, chair,
floor and pajamas. Another doughnut lay on her plate
awaiting attention. A mug full of hot chocolate, with a
marshmallow on top, stood at her elbow.

Molly eyed the breakfast and raised an eyebrow at
Alix, who took a deep breath. "I'm just so glad... If
she'd wanted caviar for breakfast I'd have gotten it for
her." There was a trace of defiance in her tone.

"Gramma was nice to give me doughnuts," Bailey added. Her voice was thick with powdered sugar.

So we have a new alliance forming, Molly thought. But that was as it should be. A grandparent and a grandchild teaming up against the generation in the middle could be healthy once in a while.

Alix's gaze wavered, and that small sign of uncertainty tugged at Molly. Maybe Megan was right, she thought. Her mother was trying, but didn't know how to break the ice.

Molly reached into the doughnut box. "Oh, why not? Everybody needs to be hyperactive once in a while, and I'll need all the energy I can muster to work today. Put another spoonful of sugar in your coffee, Mom, and join us."

Alix sat down, her spine straight and her body stiff. "Surely you're not taking Bailey to Oakwood today?"

"Why not? She'll have to learn the rules, so why not do it while the memories are still strong? Besides, the longer you just think about things the worse they get."

That philosophy, she thought, applied to her every bit as well as it did to Bailey. She couldn't avoid Luke, so her best move was to face him as soon as possible, act just as she normally would and wait to see how he intended to approach the problem.

Alix was studying Bailey's face. The child was intent on her hot chocolate, repeatedly submerging the marshmallow in an effort to melt it. "I expect you're right."

Molly dropped her doughnut.

"And I suppose the less everybody makes of this incident," Alix said thoughtfully, "the more likely she is to be all right and not turn into a spoiled brat."

"Precisely." Molly could hardly get the word out.

"In other words," Alix said, "no more doughnuts for breakfast, Bailey."

Molly hadn't recovered from the shock of having her mother agree with her by the time Watkins opened

Oakwood's front door for them. She'd never seen such a sunny look as the one he fixed on Bailey or seen a dog go into ecstasy as Lucky did when she spotted her playmate. Bailey, calmly taking the homage as her due, peeled off her jacket, dropped it in the precise center of the floor and held out her arm for Watkins to inspect the faint mark—already starting to bruise—where the intravenous needle had been.

Upstairs in the makeshift office, Warren listened patiently to Bailey's fractured account of her hospital experience. And when she went off with Mrs. Ekberg to be delivered to the kitchen, he leaned back in his chair with a sigh and said, "I'm so thankful that she's safe."

But that was all. So, Molly thought, whatever Luke might have told his father about the episode, he hadn't dropped the biggest bombshell.

But why should she have expected any other result? She should have known he'd react this way—with cynicism and disbelief.

In fact, she admitted, she *had* known it. That was why she'd sworn, long before Bailey was born, never to tell him. Only shock had made her break her vow of silence last night, with results she could have—should have—predicted. He was going to take her at her word and convince himself that the whole thing had been a nightmare woven in her overwrought mind.

At mid-afternoon, after the third time she'd had to ask Warren to repeat himself, he pointed across the room at the out-of-place hospital bed and said sternly, "It's your nap time, young woman."

Molly was too strung out to argue even if she could have mustered a logical line of reasoning. As she collapsed on the bed, she heard Warren mutter in satisfaction, "And Mrs. Ekberg wanted me to send this back to the attic. Ha!"

He was nowhere to be seen when she woke, and the room was dim. Molly stretched and sat up. The day had been a complete loss, she thought. She might as well get Bailey and go home.

She found Mrs. Ekberg dusting in the drawing room. "I'm going to call it a day," Molly said. "Where's Bailey?"

The housekeeper's duster paused. "She's not here."

Dread gnawed at Molly's stomach.

"Mr. Luke took her with him," Mrs. Ekberg said. "I assumed he'd told you because he went upstairs before he left, and when he came down he just announced that they were going out."

Molly raised her voice. "And did he happen to announce where he was going, or when he'd be back?"

From the hallway, Luke said, "As a matter of fact, I didn't."

Bailey bounded across the hallway with Lucky at her heels. "Look, Mommy! Luke made me a new badge! It's ever so much better than the one I lost!"

"It's lovely, dear. Would you go out to the kitchen for a minute with Mrs. Ekberg, please?"

They stood in silence till the childish voice and the click of the dog's claws were muffled by the kitchen door.

"That's quite the air of authority you have," Luke said, "dismissing not only the child but the staff. I didn't realize you'd been given free rein to issue orders around here."

Molly ignored him. "I'd like an explanation."

"Of what? When I thought about it, I realized you were right—the badge wasn't really the problem. So I took her down to the plant to make a new one. End of story."

"I'd decided that was to be one of the consequences of her disobedience yesterday. It was Bailey's doing that she lost her badge, and she wasn't going to get a new one for a long while."

"And I happen to think having a new one might

lessen the chances that she'll wander off toward the lake
again looking for the one she lost. Do you want to make
a federal case of it?''

"You had no right, Luke—"

"Oh, but I do." His voice was low, but there was an
edge to it like polished steel. "I have it on the best
authority that I'm her father. And that gives me all the
rights I choose to take."

Molly closed her eyes in pain. She had no one to
blame but herself. She had cut the ground from under
her own feet with that ill-advised confidence last night.

"Molly, why didn't you tell me long ago?" The edge
was still in his voice, but it was marginally less threatening.

She didn't answer right away. She was remembering
the day in his office when she'd seen him for the first
time since Megan's wedding. She had looked at him—
elegant, professional, calm, self-assured, without so
much as a shadow in his eyes to show that he remembered the night they had reached out to each other. She
had looked at the man who was Bailey's father and she
had known that she could stand there in his office and
tell him about his daughter and he wouldn't believe her.
So she hadn't.

She wet her lips and admitted, "I never intended to
tell you at all. Last night was a mistake."

"A very big mistake, Molly, from your point of
view."

"Can't you see? I was doing my best to be fair!"

"What about four and a half years ago? Did you give
any thought to fairness then? No—you never even gave
me a chance to know her. You deliberately kept her
away from me. Well, now that I know, I want my daughter, Molly. And I am going to keep her."

CHAPTER EIGHT

LUKE'S words, low and fierce, seemed to bounce off the drawing room walls like billiard balls. *I am going to keep her....*

"Closing your eyes and covering up your ears isn't going to change the situation," he said. "Stop acting like an ostrich."

Molly realized he was right. She was standing in the middle of the room with her hands cupped over her ears as if to shut out what she didn't want to hear. And not only was that kind of reaction not going to alter the facts, the display of fear was only going to encourage him to renew—maybe even expand—his demands.

Except, she thought, it was impossible to expand this particular threat. There was nothing larger, nothing worse than taking her daughter away.

She folded her hands on the back of a Chippendale side chair and tried to regain the ground she'd lost. "You can't have her," she said. Her voice shook, and she had to stop and swallow hard. "You can't take her away from me. You'd have to prove I was an unfit mother—and you can't do it."

"Sure of that, are you? You don't even have a home of your own."

"You don't, either. Warren told me himself he still owns this house. You're living on the goodwill of your father just the same way I am right now. The difference is, I'm planning to move out just as soon as I can."

"As soon as you can afford it? That's another interesting point. The matter of your job—"

"What does that mean?" she asked angrily. "Are you

129

planning to get rid of me just to improve your case? And on what grounds? How are you going to explain to your father that I've suddenly become inadequate to do my work?''

''I'm not planning anything of the sort. But you must admit your new business—with its one client—isn't going to look terribly promising to a judge.''

She wasn't listening. ''And as long as we're on the subject, what about your father, Luke? You haven't even told him, have you? He has no idea the little girl he was holding on his lap today is his grandchild. Which means that your threat is a pretty empty one.''

''I should think with the interest you have in keeping your job that you wouldn't want him to have another shock just now. You were the one who insisted he not even know Bailey was missing—''

''He'll have to face the shock sometime, won't he? Unless, of course, you just forget about this wild idea of yours altogether.''

''You'd like that, wouldn't you? Well, you're not going to get your wish.'' Luke turned on his heel. ''Just to satisfy you, I'll go drop the news on him right now. Perhaps you'd like to come along in case he needs soothing. I'm sure you'd be happy to play the angel of mercy.''

He didn't wait for an answer before he stalked out of the room.

In the sudden silence, Molly's hands clenched on the back of the chair as if she was trying to squeeze it into pieces. Once again, she thought, he had turned things against her—though this time, she admitted, she'd handed him the opportunity on a platter. She'd incited him. And if, when Warren heard this announcement, he had another relapse, it would be as much her fault as Luke's.

Luke tapped once at the door of the temporary office next to Warren's bedroom and went in. The lights were off and the room was silent.

He stood there for a moment, letting his eyes adjust to the dimness. Despite the incongruous furnishings and the passage of years, the sitting room was still permeated with his mother's presence, and gradually, under the influence of that gentle atmosphere, he felt his anger seep away.

It hadn't truly been anger, anyway, he admitted. Yes, he'd been furious with Molly, but mostly he'd been apprehensive about Warren. He wasn't afraid of how his father would react, exactly. Luke was a grown man, and he was taking full responsibility for his actions. Warren couldn't ask any more than that.

But he dreaded seeing the hurt in Warren's eyes and knowing that his carelessness had caused that pain. And so, without even understanding why, he had almost gone to his father in defiance, with something like adolescent bravado—which would have made it all so much harder for Warren.

"Thanks, Mom," he said under his breath, and stepped into the hall.

Through the stair railing he could see Mrs. Ekberg, just closing the front door. *Molly didn't waste any time in getting clear,* he thought. Though he didn't exactly blame her. Warren wasn't likely to be too pleased with her, either. Luke wondered if she'd considered how that might affect her job.

Mrs. Ekberg started up the stairs. Luke waited till she reached the top and asked, "Do you happen to know where my father is?"

"In the sun room, I believe." She looked past him and clicked her tongue. "I do wish he'd let me straighten up this room."

"It doesn't really matter, does it, Mrs. Ekberg? There are plenty of other rooms." *And putting the old furniture in place won't bring Mother back,* he thought, *it'll only make the memories stronger.* Which, he suspected, was why Warren was so stubborn about it. He moved to the top of the stairs.

"I know. It's my pride that stings, I suppose, at seeing it look so ratty. It was such a pretty room once, and your mother loved it so." She pulled the door closed with an air of finality. "Though of course as long as Miss Molly needs it for an office… It's worth any amount of injury to my pride to have her here. She's so good for Mr. Warren. He laughs again, you know."

"I know." *But he may not be laughing after I give him this news.*

He wondered what had drawn Warren to the sun room at this hour. It wasn't at its best in the afternoon. It was a room for mornings, when sunshine spilled through the long windows and emphasized the brilliant colors of flowers and birds in the gardens.

Of course, it was a fittingly ironic place for this talk, Luke thought, for it was to the sun room that he'd taken Molly the day of his mother's funeral for the chat that had been intended as apology but ended as lecture, instead.

Warren was sitting in a wicker chair so large that it made him look even more frail, his back to the windows, a book open on his lap and the dog sprawled at his feet.

Luke stopped in the doorway. "May I have a minute, Dad?"

Warren put his finger between the pages to mark his place and closed the book. "Of course. Minnesota history's been around a long time. It can wait for me a bit longer."

Luke settled on the arm of a sofa. "I have something to tell you that I'm afraid may come as a shock."

Warren looked at him, his expression politely inquiring.

As gently as he could, Luke said, "Little Bailey…

Well, she can't be my stepsister. Because she's my daughter.''

Warren didn't even blink.

The silence stretched painfully. *Didn't he understand?* "Did you hear me, Dad?"

"I'm not deaf, Lucas." Warren sounded testy. "But you said I might be shocked. I was waiting for you to get to the shocking part."

Luke's head was reeling. "That... that was it."

"Well, I hate to question your judgment, but if you truly expected me to be surprised, I'm very disappointed in you. Hadn't you noticed how much Bailey looks like your mother? It's mostly the shape of her face, I think— and perhaps the eyes, as well. I caught it the first time I saw her."

Luke hit the heel of his hand against his temple. "Let me get this straight." He couldn't keep the sarcasm out of his voice. "Do you go around checking out every kid you see in case there might be a resemblance?"

"Oh, no. Under the circumstances, I was looking for it."

Luke felt as if he'd regrouped from the first sucker punch just in time to be hit with another. Why would his father have considered the possibility when Luke himself hadn't even been suspicious?

"That day I interviewed Molly," Warren went on, sounding pleased with himself, "she was very nervous when you showed up. And she didn't answer the question when I asked if you and she had been friends. I just...wondered." His voice picked up a tart edge. "Of course as time's gone on, I wondered even more whether anyone was going to admit it."

"I didn't know, Dad. Believe me. If I had—"

If I had known, what would I have done? He'd have shouldered his responsibility for his child, of course. But beyond that...

It was easy to look back through rose-colored glasses

and create some happy-ever-after scenario. But the fact was they'd been a couple of careless kids caught in a passionate moment. Molly had been suffering from a massive infatuation. Luke had never before seen her as anything but the kid who tagged along and too often had to be rescued. It was hardly a blueprint for any kind of long-term relationship.

How long would it have been before her infatuation burned itself out in day-to-day contact and left her bitterly blaming him? How long would it have been before he grew to resent that she'd had to be rescued once more?

Not that any of those things mattered, of course. Trying to figure out what might have happened in the past if things had been different was pure fiction. It was the present that had to be dealt with.

Luke said, softly, "I don't know what to do, Dad."

Nothing interrupted the silence except the scrape of a stray branch against the glass.

Finally Warren leaned forward and patted Luke's arm. "I'm not worried about that," he said. "You'll do the right thing, I'm certain." He smiled reassuringly and pushed himself up from his chair, and left Luke sitting there alone.

Even with the fits and starts of the last few days, the book was progressing nicely. Warren was obviously pleased with the project. He read the new section Molly had finished that morning and set it aside with a contented sigh. "I can't think of a single way to improve it," he said. "We seem to be on exactly the same wavelength, Molly."

Hardly, Molly thought. *Because if you knew what I was thinking...*

She'd had to force herself to walk into Oakwood that afternoon for her first encounter with Warren since Luke had talked to him. He'd been waiting for her in the dining room. She sent Bailey straight to the kitchen, squared her shoulders and went in to face him. But Warren's demeanor hadn't changed at all. Over lunch he told her about the volume of history he'd been reading with the same gentle, self-deprecating humor he'd shown so many times before.

She'd been seriously off balance until she realized that he wouldn't mention such a sensitive subject where some of the staff might overhear. He'd wait till they were alone.

But even when they'd gone up to the sitting room where no one could intrude, he said nothing.

Luke lost his nerve, Molly thought, and told herself it was stupid to feel disappointed—for wasn't that exactly what she wanted?

She pushed the question aside. She'd have the rest of her life to sort out the answer. "Now that we've got an overview of all of Meditronics' history," she said, "I think we should start playing with the video idea. What do we want it to look like?"

Warren's brow wrinkled. "I thought it would just follow along the same path as the book."

"It could. That way it would be something like a fast-paced slide show. Or we could present it as—"

She was interrupted by a soft knock, and a moment later Bailey's face appeared around the edge of the door. She clutched a basket piled high with aromatic golden-brown scones, and two steps behind her was Mrs. Ekberg with a tea tray.

"Cook made scones so Bailey could practice her measuring," the housekeeper explained, "and we decided to share the wealth. I hope we're not interrupting, but they're best when they're fresh and hot. And you two need a break now and then, anyway."

Bailey set the basket squarely atop her mother's papers and bounded across the room to fling herself at Warren. "I didn't get to show you my ouch today," she told him and held out her arm to display the bruised spot where the IV needle had been. But as soon as he'd sympathized, she slid off his lap and tugged at Mrs. Ekberg's sleeve. "I'm ready to go. Come play tea with me."

As the door closed behind them, Molly shook her head in wonder. "She made scones just so Bailey could measure the ingredients? Your staff is the limit, Warren. Furthermore, I'll bet Bailey decided to use the silver tea service today, and that's the only reason we got the Haviland one."

Warren didn't answer.

Molly glanced at him and was startled to see the brilliance of tears in his eyes.

He wiped them away and said, "Thank you, my dear. I'm so glad to have the chance to know my beautiful granddaughter."

Molly felt as if she was being choked. "He told you, then," she managed to say.

Warren nodded. "My only regret is how long it took."

"I'm sorry," Molly said. Conscience, shrieking that she must be fair, pushed her on. "That isn't Luke's fault. He didn't know." She bit her lip and added under her breath, "And now that he does, he's plenty angry about it."

Warren split a scone and spread jam across the steaming surface. "Lucas is generally pretty levelheaded. Give him a little time, and I expect he'll come around." He looked up and smiled. "Now, tell me what Miss B was like as a baby."

The reminiscences, and Warren's reaction to them, left Molly feeling almost buoyant when she came downstairs to collect Bailey an hour later. There was no doubt where to find her. The child was sitting on the bottom step next to Luke, holding a new doll and surrounded by heaps of tiny, exquisite doll clothes—a wardrobe that made Molly's look sparse.

Suddenly she wasn't flying high any more. She felt like a week-old helium balloon. Yesterday it had been the badge. Today he'd escalated to a doll. At the rate he was going, Luke's little princess was very quickly going to become a spoiled brat whining for a present every time she saw him.

Bailey looked blissful. "Look, Mommy, what Luke brought me."

"I see," Molly said. She stepped across the sea of doll clothes and faced Luke squarely. "I believe I need to talk to you."

"And I have a few things to bring to your attention, too." He stood up, and Molly thought of a rattlesnake uncoiling just enough to strike. "I've made arrangements with Mrs. Ekberg for Bailey to stay with her so we can go out for an early dinner."

"I'd sooner eat grass."

"We could stay here, of course. But this conversation is likely to take a while, and unless you'd enjoy having my father's input into the discussion—"

Molly glared at him. "Obviously I don't have a choice. So yes, I'd love to have dinner with you."

"That's what I thought," Luke murmured. "Mrs. Ekberg will put Bailey to bed here, and she can stay the night."

Molly didn't need a guidebook to see the logic behind that suggestion. He was starting to lay the foundations for his custody case. It would look good to a judge for Bailey to already be spending nights at Oakwood.

"Absolutely not," Molly said. "She can put her to bed—if we're gone that long, which I doubt will be the case. But I'll take her home with me. I won't leave her alone."

"She won't be alone. And we might as well start making the transition."

She could hardly believe her ears. "*What* transition?

If that's what you want to talk to me about, don't get the idea that a steak will change my mind."

"I'm of the opinion," he said gently, "that nothing short of a stick of dynamite would change your mind."

And what exactly does that mean? Before Molly had a chance to dissect the statement, he'd picked Bailey up for a hug. "I'm taking your mother out on a dinner date, princess. Be good for Mrs. Ekberg, all right?"

Bailey's lower lip crept out. "I want to go."

"Do you? Maybe I'll take you next time." He held her while she leaned out of his arms to give her mother a kiss, then turned her over to Mrs. Ekberg.

"Don't think I missed that," Molly said acidly as he swept her out the front door to the Jaguar. "The little maneuver where you didn't even let me hold her to kiss her goodbye."

Luke raised his eyebrows, but didn't comment, just opened the passenger door for her.

Molly settled herself and folded her arms tightly. "You are not taking her away from me," she said as Luke slid behind the wheel.

"Molly, sometimes you sound like a broken record."

"And I'll keep right on until you understand what I'm saying. Another thing, Luke—the incredible toys have to stop."

"One doll," he said. "This is hardly a crime."

"It looked like Christmas in that hallway."

He glanced at her. "Obviously you've never experienced an Oakwood Christmas."

"Your family traditions are beside the point. If you try to buy her, you'll destroy her, Luke."

He didn't comment, and in a few minutes the Jaguar stopped in front of one of the most elegant restaurants in the city.

Great, Molly thought. *My one chance to come here, and not only does it have to be with Luke, but I didn't even have a minute to freshen my lipstick.*

Luke helped her out, a valet took charge of the car, and a uniformed doorman ushered them inside.

It was early, and the dining room, which looked over the deep blue water of Lake Superior, was almost empty. The maître d' showed them to a table in an isolated corner and fussed over seating Molly so she had the best view of the lake.

Perhaps his idea of going out for dinner hadn't been so crazy after all, Molly thought. On a weeknight, in this quiet place, they were not likely to be disturbed. On the other hand, anything she tried to eat was apt to choke her. Luke seemed to understand that. He didn't ask what she'd like for an appetizer, he simply ordered.

"I don't intend to drown her in gifts," Luke said, "just provide a few things—"

"A few things?"

"That will make her feel…comfortable at Oakwood."

She knew he'd almost said *at home* but had thought better of it at the last moment.

Luke leaned forward. His eyes were so dark and intense she couldn't meet his gaze any longer. "Molly, I want to tell her I'm her father."

She stared at her menu as if it was the most interesting piece of literature in the world. "I'm sure you don't need my permission."

"I'd like to have your help."

She slapped the menu shut and flung it on the table. "You're threatening to take my daughter away from me, and you want me to help you do it?"

"Not exactly." Luke looked past Molly and nodded, and the wine steward approached the table.

By the time Luke had approved the wine, Molly had managed to regain her self-control.

"The wine's very good," he said. "Try some, it'll help you relax."

"I don't want to relax. To answer your question, Luke—"

"She's going to be told. Would you rather be there to answer her questions and help her adjust or not?"

Molly bit her lip. He knew perfectly well she couldn't deliberately hurt Bailey. He'd neatly boxed her in. She had no real choice.

Obviously he knew it, but instead of closing in for the kill as she'd expected, Luke sat back in his chair. The only sign of nerves she could see was that he held his wineglass by the stem and was endlessly turning it, staring at the deep red liquid as it sloshed in rhythm with the movement of his fingers. "I talked to my attorney today."

She hadn't expected him to move quite so fast—or, having done so, to give her warning. "And?" she asked cautiously.

"He feels my chances of getting custody aren't very good."

His voice was very quiet, and it took Molly an instant to register the importance of the words. "But that's—"

Before hope could rush over her, he snatched it away. "Except, of course, that I have far more resources than you do, and I can wear you down until you can't afford to fight me any more, and I'll win by default."

She drew a long, slow, shaky breath, which burned her throat worse than raw alcohol would. "That's not fair."

The waiter set a tray between them. Luke picked up his wineglass and looked at her over the rim. "And you have been fair to me?"

Molly put her face into her cupped hands. She had made a very big mistake. He'd told her so. She suspected she was only beginning to understand how huge her miscalculation had been.

"Do try the pâté," Luke murmured. "I think you'll enjoy it. I've found it to be the best anywhere in the city."

The only way she would enjoy the pâté, Molly

thought, was if she pushed his face into it. But surely she didn't have to sit still for this torture. "I'm sure it's lovely," she said icily. "But I don't seem to be hungry, after all. If you'll excuse me—"

"Sit down."

"Why?"

"Because we've only started. You're quite right—bankrupting you wouldn't be fair. More to the point, it would take longer than I care to wait."

If he knew the state of her resources, Molly thought, he might change his mind about that. She sank into her chair.

Luke spread pâté on a toast point and held it out to her. "So I'm offering you a compromise."

"I'm listening." Absentmindedly, she took the tidbit.

"Joint custody."

"Which means precisely what? Half her time with you, half with me? I'm not agreeing to that, you understand, just asking."

"Some families handle it that way. It wouldn't be my first choice. In legal terms, joint custody means we both retain full parental rights to the child. What it comes down to is that neither of us makes decisions about her without the approval of the other."

"And judging by the way we've agreed on everything so far," Molly said sweetly, "that ought to be positively enjoyable. Do you mean major decisions or any at all? If I'd have to consult you before I get her hair cut—"

"Major decisions." He looked at her approvingly. "I'm glad you're enjoying the pâté. Would you care for another?"

Molly hadn't been aware that she'd eaten it, but her hand was empty.

He carefully created another tidbit and passed it to her. "For instance, you couldn't move back to Chicago with her unless I agreed to it."

Molly hadn't even considered the idea. Suddenly it looked horribly attractive.

"In practical terms," Luke went on, "it would mean Bailey will continue to live with you, at least for now—but I'd have unrestricted contact. None of this every-other-weekend-and-three-hours-on-Wednesdays sort of nonsense."

"*At least for now?* And what precisely does that mean?"

"It means," Luke said levelly, "when she's a few years older, she can make up her own mind where she lives."

"And you'll no doubt make sure she has all the goodies in the meantime, so she'll choose you."

"I don't happen to think she's quite that easily manipulated, Molly, and I know I'm not that stupid. In any case, you aren't going to be hard-pressed for cash yourself. My attorney also told me what I could expect a court to order in child support under a joint custody arrangement. So I'll start writing you a check every month." He held out another toast point.

"No." She reached across the table and pushed his hand back. Her palm felt as if it had been scalded by the brief contact. "I will not live on your money."

He ignored her. "I've also started an account into which I'll deposit the amount I'd have paid over the last four years."

Molly gritted her teeth and fought a battle with her pride. She had supported her daughter for nearly four years and she could continue to do so. But was it fair to Bailey to turn down the sort of security his nest egg would represent? "All right," she said reluctantly. "But I want you to know right now that I won't draw a dollar out of it. It'll be Bailey's college fund."

Luke shrugged. "Dad's already taken care of that. He made the arrangements this morning. Those are my terms, Molly. My name goes on her birth certificate. We agree to joint custody. We have an equal voice in what happens to her. I have free access to her any time. And of course I pay child support.''

"And if I don't agree, you take me to court.''

Luke said genially, ''And wear you down until you can't afford to fight any more.''

"That's blackmail, Luke.''

"I prefer to think of it as the stick of dynamite it takes to change your mind.'' He picked up his wineglass. "It's reality, Molly. Make your choice.''

But she had none, and both of them knew it. Molly took a deep breath and nodded.

Luke raised his wineglass. "To our daughter. When shall we tell her, do you think?''

Luke was more nervous about facing a three-year-old than he'd been in any other situation in his life. Being called on the carpet during his teenage years, watching his first autopsy in medical school, committing himself to a ten-million-dollar deal—none of them could compare.

It didn't help that their conversation with Bailey had to be put off till the next day. She'd been asleep when they got back to Oakwood, and Molly said, "It won't do any good to try to wake her, because she wouldn't remember a thing.''

So he had reluctantly carried his drowsy daughter to Molly's car and spent the night rehearsing what he'd say to her.

They'd agreed to take her for a drive up the lakeshore late the following afternoon, to a beach where there would be complete privacy and no interruptions. That had been Molly's suggestion. Luke suspected it was because she had no more idea how Bailey might react than he did. She'd never admit it, though. He was certain of that.

He went home early and changed into jeans and running shoes, but when he went to the makeshift office to see when Molly would be free, he was startled to find the door open, the enormous desk in pieces in the hallway and Mrs. Ekberg stripping the sheets off the hospital bed. "What happened?" he asked.

The housekeeper shrugged. "Don't ask me. He called a crew in to move most of the boxes to the storage room and told me he was well enough now to work in the library, so I could do what I liked in here. I thought I'd better leap at the chance."

"I can see that," Luke said.

"*And* he told me to make up the green bedroom at the far end of the hall for him because he's moving down there."

"What? Why's he giving up his bedroom?"

"That's what I asked him. He just gave me that look of his that tells you to mind your own business and went off. He was whistling," Mrs. Ekberg added darkly. "Miss Molly said to tell you she'd be with you in a few minutes."

"Thanks," Luke said absently.

He found his father in the library with a legal document spread out on the desk blotter.

"Molly's changing her clothes," Warren said.

"I heard. Mrs. Ekberg thinks you've flipped."

"Why?"

"Because the master of the house is moving out of the master suite, that's why."

"Oh, that." He tapped the document. "I'm deeding the house over to you."

Luke's heart plunged to his toes. "Dad—you're not that sick. Are you?"

"Doesn't matter, it's time. So since I'm not going to be the owner anymore, I'm vacating the main bedroom." He added airily, "You'll notice, however, that before I sign the papers I'm settling myself firmly in a room just down the hall.'' He grinned and laid the document aside. "So what are you and Molly up to today?"

You and Molly. So that was the way the wind had shifted. Well, Warren would get the message sooner or later that Luke and Molly weren't a combination and weren't ever going to be.

"Luke!" Bailey called, and flung herself on him. He tossed her over his shoulder like a sack of grain and let his gaze roam over her mother. He'd been right about the jeans, he decided. With her long, slim legs Molly looked great in them. Though there might be other outfits that would do as well...

"Don't get any ideas, Warren." Molly's voice was crisp.

Luke frowned. Did she need to be quite so curt? Surely there was no need to fuss about Warren's crazy notions right now.

"Haven't had an idea in years," Warren murmured. "Have a good time—whatever you have planned."

They drove a few miles up the scenic highway toward Two Harbors and pulled off to walk along a deserted pebbly beach to look for agates. A little later, Molly sat on a driftwood log, cuddled Bailey close beside her and told the child that she now had the father she'd asked for.

Bailey looked from her mother to Luke. Her face was solemn, her forehead wrinkled as if she didn't quite understand. "You're going to be my daddy?"

Luke nodded. He felt as if he was taking a vow. As carefully as if she were a bubble, he stretched out a forefinger to touch his daughter's hand. "I'm very proud to be your daddy, Bailey."

Bailey's face cleared. "Okay." She bounced from her seat on the log, opened her sweaty little hand and dumped her trove of agates into Luke's palm. "I'm ready to go," she announced. "I want a date supper."

"Dinner date," Molly corrected, but Bailey was gone,

plunging across the sand toward where they'd left the car.

Bewildered, Luke looked at Molly. "That's it?" he murmured. "That's all she's got to say about it?"

"What else is there?" She stood up and dusted off the seat of her jeans. "Congratulations, Mr. Hudson. You're a father."

He knew she'd meant the words to be ironic, but somewhere in the middle her voice caught. He spotted tears as she turned away.

He didn't know how to comfort her. He didn't even know if he wanted to try. After all, it wasn't as if he'd robbed her of her child. The whole point was that he didn't intend to.

Still, she'd been incredibly generous, handling the situation as she had. She could have made it all very difficult.

"Molly." He put his arm around her shoulders and was startled at how small and fragile she felt.

For a moment she stood still, her head bent, her face turned but pressed against his arm. Then she stepped away from him and walked to the car. She looked very much alone.

Luke lifted Bailey into her safety seat. "Now, how about that dinner date? Where are we going?"

She looked at him as if he'd sprung a cog and said, "KidzPlace."

Luke raised an eyebrow and turned to Molly. "She sounds as if there's nowhere else."

"There isn't, in her mind." Molly fastened her seat belt.

He was mildly annoyed that she hadn't looked at him even once since she'd sat with Bailey on the driftwood log.

"If you'll just drop me at Oakwood before you go to the restaurant, Luke—"

Bailey said, "I want Mommy, too."

He saw a flicker of pain cross Molly's face. "Honey, sometimes… Sometimes Daddy wants to just be with you."

It hurt her to say that, he thought. But she'd done it anyway. For Bailey's sake, of course, but still…

Bailey thrust lower lip out.

"But this isn't one of those times," Luke said. "Of course your mommy's going too, princess."

"Please don't, Luke." Her voice was so low he had to lean toward her to hear. "Don't encourage her to believe that we're a family—because we're not."

"We're going to have a hamburger, Molly," he said dryly. "Not a major life-style change."

She didn't say any more. But she still didn't look at him.

Between her rubbery chicken bits and KidzPlace's enormous indoor playground, Bailey was in heaven. She climbed over, under and around, now and then calling, "Look at me!" and beaming when they applauded.

"Little daredevil," Luke said. "She's really something, isn't she? I wish—" He stopped abruptly. "I wish I could be more than a part-time dad."

Molly stared at him. "Don't try it," she said harshly. "You made an agreement and you have no choice but to follow through with it."

"Do I?" he asked, almost to himself. "What if there's a different way? A better way?"

He saw the fear that filled her eyes—the fear that she would lose her daughter. And he felt the same fear deep in his gut.

Warren's words rang in his ears. *You'll do the right thing,* he'd said. *I'm sure of it.* And he'd moved out of the master bedroom and restored the room next door, as if he expected…

Don't encourage her to believe that we're a family, Molly had said a little while ago.

But why not?

Luke looked into his empty coffee cup, then across the table at the mother of his child. And he heard himself say, as if from a great distance, "Will you marry me?"

CHAPTER NINE

MOLLY'S hand went numb with shock, and almost in slow motion, her coffee cup tipped onto its side. She didn't realize it till the barely warm dregs dripped on her jeans and soaked through to her skin. She reached for a napkin to blot the spill, but the action was automatic. She was incapable of thinking.

Will you marry me?

What in heaven's name was the man up to now? He couldn't actually mean it, could he? Just a few minutes ago he'd said he had no intention of embarking on a major life-style change.

Her paper napkin turned brown and soggy, and Luke went after another handful from the service counter. As Molly finished mopping the mess he picked up his own empty cup and said, "Would you like some more coffee?"

He sounded, Molly thought, as if the question was just as important as the last one he'd asked. "No, thanks."

Luke sat down. "You're right. It tastes pretty bad, doesn't it?"

She watched his long fingers as he fiddled with the paper cup. He folded the handles and unrolled the rim. She looked on in fascination, wondering if he realized what he was doing.

"As nervous as you are about it," she said finally, "perhaps you'd like to pretend you didn't ask that question. And I don't mean the one about the coffee."

Luke didn't answer. He seemed to be thinking it over.

Time stood still. Molly waited, trying not to hold her breath, trying to tell herself that it really didn't matter

149

whether he was thinking better of a few rash words. But she knew it did matter. She didn't want him to withdraw the question because—despite the years and the pain— she still cared for him.

No, that wasn't quite accurate. She didn't care for him *still.* She'd learned to care for him *again.*

Once, as a girl, she had worshipped him and thought it was the same as being in love. Now she knew the difference, and now she knew it wasn't infatuation she felt.

Because she had left behind that schoolgirl crush, she had foolishly believed she had gotten over Luke. Instead, in the past weeks, as she had come to know the man he had become, something far more lasting had awakened deep inside her.

She had fallen in love with him. She had done so blindly, heedlessly, foolishly—but no less certainly.

Looking back, she had no trouble at all diagnosing what had happened to her. She even knew the moment it had started—that very first day in his office, when she'd seen how worried Luke was about his father and the lengths he was willing to go to reawaken Warren's interest in life. And then there was the way he'd treated Bailey from the very beginning. How many men would have postponed the start of a business day to make a silly badge for a three-year-old? Or put aside exhaustion to teach her how to play with a dog as large as she was?

Molly had been tiptoeing along a precipice long be- fore the night Bailey had been lost—but that was no doubt when she'd gone over the edge for good. She'd been so horribly upset, and Luke had been there like a rock, holding her steady and keeping her safe as surely as the dog had protected Bailey.

Even in the midst of her distress, how could she have failed to recognize that her reaction to him wasn't simple gratitude but something a great deal more complicated?

Subconsciously, she must have known—and she had

not wanted to let go of him even when the danger was past. So she'd blurted out the truth about his daughter—not only because it wouldn't have been fair not to tell him but because she wanted to hold onto Luke.

She had wanted...this.

"A little nervous yourself, aren't you?" Luke said.

Molly realized she'd turned the last dry napkin into infinitesimal shreds. Awkwardly, she bundled the evidence inside the coffee-logged wad of paper, propped her elbows on the table and folded her hands.

Luke said, "We aren't going to pretend I didn't ask, because I did. And the question stands."

It didn't only stand, Molly thought, it positively resounded. She was surprised Bailey hadn't heard it all the way up at the top of the playground.

Will you marry me?

But that wasn't truly what he was asking, she knew. At its heart, the question really had nothing to do with her. If it wasn't for Bailey, the thought of marrying Molly would never have crossed Luke's mind, and they both knew it.

All she had to do was say yes and she would have achieved exactly what she'd subconsciously set out to do. But only now did Molly realize how hollow the accomplishment would be. He didn't want to marry her, but he'd go through the motions. To have his child all the time, to be more than a makeshift dad, to give Bailey the semblance of a normal family, he would make the sacrifice of marrying her mother.

"For Bailey." Molly managed to keep her voice level.

Luke glanced at the playground. Molly followed his gaze and watched Bailey come down the plastic-tube slide headfirst.

He sounded impatient. "Of course it's for Bailey. I never said this would be the love match of the century."

His tone, as much as the words, scraped Molly's soul

raw. "I certainly can't argue with that." *Because even though I love you, you don't love me.*

He shrugged. "I thought we were actually getting along fairly well for a while until this little difficulty came up."

"This little difficulty?"

"Deciding who gets Bailey. If we don't have to argue about that, I don't see any reason we couldn't deal reasonably well together."

It was a chilly assessment of what would undoubtedly be an even cooler relationship.

I have to say no, Molly told herself. *It will only hurt worse, and longer, if I don't.* But even though she knew it would be a disaster if she agreed, she couldn't force herself to turn down what she wanted so badly. Not directly. She did the best she could. "Luke, listen to yourself. It's crazy."

"Is it? If you'd told me at Megan's wedding about the baby, and I'd proposed, you'd have married me in a minute."

"I thought I loved you, then." *And now I know I do— and it doesn't make a bit of difference, because you don't care about me.* "What sort of odds would you have given that marriage?"

He didn't hesitate. "Slim to none. But we're not kids anymore, Molly. We're not blinded by infatuation."

"We're not foolish enough to think that love solves everything," she said wryly.

"Exactly—love doesn't come into it at all. And we both want what's best for Bailey."

Bailey. They'd come around in a circle. Was he right, that this alliance—she could hardly call it a marriage— was in Bailey's best interests?

Instead of being shuffled between two people, two houses, never quite knowing where she fit in, Bailey would have two full-time parents, a fairly normal family life, one home. And what a home. Not that material things could be allowed to matter in a decision as important as this.

Molly had sworn on the day Bailey was born that she would put her child's welfare above everything else, that she would never again make a decision without first considering its impact on Bailey.

But how far did that go? Was it her duty to accept Luke's proposal—for Bailey's sake?

Or would she simply be using Bailey as an excuse for doing precisely what she wanted? And fooling herself all the while not only about her motives but their chances of success?

She was certain of only one thing—that she was too confused to make a rational decision. "I need some time to think about it, Luke."

"Molly, there have been peace treaties that were negotiated faster than this."

Under different circumstances, Molly thought, the edge in his voice might have sounded like the desperation of a young man deeply in love and afraid he was going to be turned down. At least he'd been honest. She was glad of that.

Bailey appeared at her elbow, her face flushed from exercise and her hair damp with perspiration. "Mommy, I want something to drink."

Molly reached across the table for her plastic milk glass.

"How long do you want?" Luke asked.

"Everything's changed so fast, Luke. Surely it isn't asking too much to take a few days to think it over."

"All right. But I'm not going to accept some vague I'll-let-you-know-whenever-I've-decided nonsense, so set a time."

"You really think I want to leave something like this hanging over my head indefinitely?" She sighed. "My parents' anniversary party is a week from Saturday. How's that?"

"I suppose it'll do. And if you make up your mind before then—"

"Believe me," Molly said, "you'll be the first to know."

Bailey fell asleep in her car seat on the drive home, worn out by her antics at the beach and on the playground, and she hardly stirred when Luke lifted her, seat and all, from the Jaguar and strapped her into Molly's car. Her overwhelming innocence tugged Molly's heart. *If only I could look into the future and see the best way to keep her from being hurt.*

Molly opened her car door, but she didn't get in. "We only talked about Bailey," she said, without looking at Luke. "What about...us?"

"Do you mean, am I suggesting a real marriage or something that only appears to be?"

"I guess that's what I'm asking, yes." She knew when he moved closer, for the back of her neck tingled.

His voice was very low. "I think separate bedrooms would be a little hypocritical, don't you, considering that we already have a daughter?"

Molly tried in vain to swallow the lump in her throat.

Luke's hands came to rest on her shoulders, and he turned her to face him. "Perhaps we should try a little experiment."

There was no doubt what he had in mind. The husky note in his voice would have told her even if there'd been no other signals.

Molly could hardly out-and-out refuse to let him kiss her when she'd brought up the subject herself. If she balked or didn't cooperate, he'd only ask why she was afraid of the very answers she'd asked for.

And in any case, she wanted to know.

She looked at him and closed her eyes and told herself that this would be basically the same as all the other good-night kisses she'd taken part in over the last few years. She wasn't so foolish—or so inexperienced—as to think that one kiss was exactly like another, but at the heart of the matter Luke's technique probably wasn't so very different than that of any of the men she'd dated.

The fact that he'd given her the first real kisses of her life, and the fact that the circumstances surrounding those kisses had been extremely emotional, had no doubt colored her perceptions and made each caress seem better than it had really been. There probably wasn't a man on earth who could live up to the memories she'd constructed from that long-ago night. It wasn't fair of her even to compare...

Her carefully crafted illusion lasted less than three seconds.

Luke cupped her face in his hands, ran his thumb gently across her lower lip and bent his head. He tasted her slowly and thoughtfully, his mouth barely brushing hers. She shivered uncontrollably, and she wondered how such a gentle touch could cause such violent darts of pleasure throughout her body.

He drew back slightly. "You don't like that approach? Then perhaps—in the name of experimentation—we should try another."

She wanted to say, *No, I like this one just fine.* But her vocal cords were paralyzed. That had never happened before.

Luke obviously took her silence for agreement, and his hands slid firmly over her shoulders and down her back, drawing her close until her body seemed to meld with his. Off balance, she could do nothing but cling to him while his kisses turned ravenous. He commanded her response, and when she obeyed, he demanded more and more. He took her breath, her strength, her willpower...but he gave, as well, until every nerve in her body was vibrating to his touch like the strings of a cello.

When he let her go, Molly sagged against the driver's door and tried not to gasp for air. She realized that Luke, too, was leaning against the car. Was he relying on it for support, she wondered, or simply striking a casual pose to show how unaffected he was?

"I'd consider that a success," he said. His voice was low and a little rough. "What about you, Molly?"

She gave up the struggle to regain control of her knees and sank into her seat. "Good night, Luke."

He leaned across her and solicitously fastened her seat belt. It was the first time Molly had ever considered such a utilitarian action in the light of a seduction technique, for though he didn't lay a finger on her body, his careful attention to the straps made her terribly aware that her breasts still tingled from his embrace and her stomach was simply gone.

He started to withdraw from the car and paused just long enough to press another brief butterfly of a kiss on her lips.

"Give it a chance," he murmured, "and you might get to like that one, too. Drive carefully, Molly."

The ripples of pleasure were diminishing, like the waves left behind by a rock tossed into still water, and reality was once more intruding.

She glanced in the driving mirror at Bailey, her face nestled into the cushioned car seat, sublimely unaware of a scene that would no doubt have fascinated her.

Bailey, who was the only reason he'd kissed her.

"I will," she said tightly. "I have precious cargo."

Luke raised his eyebrows a fraction. "But of course you do."

And she told herself, as she turned onto London Road, that a wise woman wouldn't forget that the entire episode had been only an investigation of whether they could stand each other well enough to form an alliance for Bailey.

Megan's maid opened the Bannisters' massive front door and stepped aside for Molly to enter. "Mrs. Bannister is in her boudoir."

"Thanks. I can find my way." Molly stopped halfway up the elegant staircase and looked over the huge atrium where a week from tomorrow her parents would celebrate their anniversary.

The day she must give Luke his answer.

But that was utter nonsense, of course. She'd lain awake half the night, and she'd concluded that she'd have to be completely mad to accept his proposal. Having made up her mind, there was no point in postponing. She'd tell him today and have it done with.

She tapped on the boudoir door and followed Megan's summons to the bedroom beyond.

Megan was lying on an enormous four-poster bed, her back propped against a stack of peach satin pillows, wearing a negligee that was more lace than anything else and holding a paperback in her hand. Molly thought she looked terribly fragile. Even her hair, brushed but left loose around her shoulders, seemed to have lost its healthy sheen.

"How was the trip yesterday?" Molly leaned over to kiss her sister's cheek.

"Dull, like most of Rand's business things. And it was a very long day, which is why I'm still in bed. When you called this morning I started to get up, but I just couldn't."

"You need to take care of yourself just now." Molly sat at the foot of the bed.

Megan's face brightened. "Anyway, I sneaked away for a couple of hours yesterday to shop. I brought home a couple of dresses for the anniversary party."

"How many are you planning to wear?"

Megan pulled her knees up and folded her arms around them. "Silly—they're for you. Obviously you haven't had time to shop. If you like what I chose— well, I missed your birthday last winter. And if you don't, I'll ship them back." She shrugged. "So please don't make a big deal of it. Looking for clothes for you was the most fun I had all day.''

If Molly had ever felt guiltier, she couldn't remember it. She had to reply to Megan's generosity with a piece of news that might cut her sister to the heart.

"Would you like some coffee or something?" Megan asked. "And you wanted to see the Waterford bowl, too."

"Can we do that later? And no coffee, thanks." Molly braced herself. "I didn't really come to see the bowl, anyway."

"Oh? This sounds promising."

Molly asked, as delicately as she could, "You haven't talked to Luke lately?"

"Not since that night in the hospital. Why?"

"Nothing, really." She'd procrastinated long enough. There was no easy way to say this, so she might as well stop hoping one would drop into her lap. "I wanted to tell you about a sort of family meeting I had with Mother and Dad the night before last. I called to see if you could come, but Rand said you'd gone to bed already to rest for the trip." She couldn't look at Megan, so her gaze wandered. She noted almost absently that the other side of the big bed had obviously not been used last night. Had Rand thoughtfully left his wife alone so he wouldn't disturb her rest? Or was this a regular thing?

And Luke didn't want separate rooms. Maybe she should tell him—with only a hint of sarcasm, of course—that all the best people had them.

Megan's fingers plucked at the hem of the peach satin sheet. "He must have forgotten to tell me you'd called." She forced a smile. "So what was so weighty it needed a family meeting? And how does Luke come into it?"

"Luke—" Molly bit her lip and looked at her hands, white-knuckled in her lap "—is Bailey's father."

Megan couldn't have looked more stunned if Molly

had picked up the marble base of the bedside lamp and hit her over the head.

Molly's stomach tied itself into a half-dozen knots. "I'm sorry," she said miserably. "I know he's very important to you." *I just hoped he wasn't quite this important.* She fumbled, trying to think of anything that might lessen Megan's shock. "Anyway, all this happened years ago, so it really doesn't affect—"

Except for the part about getting married, her conscience reminded her, and it looked as if that would affect Megan plenty. But since Molly wasn't going to marry him, after all…

"I thought maybe he'd have told you." Molly's voice trailed off.

Megan shook her head as if to clear it. "No. He's never even dropped a hint to me. That night at the hospital he even asked me about Bailey's father." Delicate color rose in her cheeks as she admitted, "I told him the little I knew and felt absolutely delinquent for talking about your secrets. When I get my hands on him—"

Molly frowned. Megan didn't sound quite as she would have expected for a woman whose world had been turned on its axis.

"I'm surprised you didn't brain me when I started talking about stepfathers," Megan muttered. "I deserved it. Here I was feeling out whether you even knew you were falling for him without so much as a suspicion that you'd already… Well!"

Molly's head was swimming. "You don't…mind?"

"Mind what? That one of my best friends doesn't tell me a teensy detail like the fact that he's my niece's father, or that my little sister didn't trust me any more than that?"

"Luke didn't know. I told him at the hospital."

"Oh, in that case, no wonder he looked as if he'd been hit by a tree."

Or a treehouse, Molly thought. She was giddy. If

Megan really didn't feel romantic about Luke... The whole thing would have been so much more unpleasant if Megan's heart was at stake, too.

Megan was sitting up straight, and there was more sparkle in her eyes than Molly had seen there in weeks. "How did Mother take it? With fireworks, or was she thrilled to pieces that her granddaughter's a Hudson? I wish I'd been there."

Molly shook her head. "Neither. It was weird, Meg. Almost scary. She looked at me and blinked twice and said something about how that might account for the graceful way Bailey moves, since Luke's mother was a dancer. That was it."

"Now I *really* wish I'd been there," Megan said. "So...what's next? With you and Luke, I mean."

"Nothing's next. The arrangements won't be any different than the ordinary divorced couple makes, really."

Megan raised her delicately plucked eyebrows. "Whatever you say, dear. But you look pretty guilty to me."

Molly felt herself color. But she was *not* going to tell Megan about Luke's proposal. What was the point in asking for trouble? Or leaving herself open to well-meant advice, which might be even worse?

She'd decided to turn him down, anyway.

Hadn't she?

Lucky was outside Oakwood that afternoon, sniffing through a flower bed, when Molly parked her car. Bailey bounced in her seat, so eager to join the dog that she made it hard to release her safety harness. But finally she was free to race off. Molly got her briefcase and the stack of books she was returning to Warren and called to the child. "Come on, Bailey, you know the rule. You can't be outside without an adult, and Lucky doesn't count."

"I'll be good," Bailey pleaded.

"I'm just making sure you remember not to wander off again."

Bailey pouted for a few seconds until she concluded her mother wasn't paying any attention, then obeyed. Three-year-olds were so delightfully transparent, Molly thought.

The child bounded to the front door, knocked confidently and swept past the butler with a cheerful, "Good afternoon, Watkins!"

Where had she picked up that one, Molly wondered.

Watkins made the required daily inspection of Bailey's yellowing bruise, then she hopped on one foot to the kitchen to greet the cook.

Bailey was so obviously happy at Oakwood, Molly thought. For the first time she considered what would happen after her work was done. The book was moving along. Most of the work on the video couldn't be done from Oakwood.

When Molly no longer came to Oakwood every afternoon, there would be no reason for Bailey to do so. Of course, come autumn she'd be spending more time in preschool, anyway—but unless Luke made it a point to take her home with him, there might be whole weeks when she didn't see her pals at Oakwood.

She would miss them. Unless…

Molly bit her lip. *Unless I marry Luke,* she thought, and all her uncertainty swirled once more.

Could she live without love? There would unquestionably be passion. After last night, there could be no doubt of that. Would it be an adequate substitute? Could she be contented knowing Bailey was happy? Would that satisfaction be enough?

And could she manage all of that…for a lifetime?

Not a day went by without a fresh jolt for Molly, and an additional argument to add to the ongoing battle in her head.

On Monday afternoon when she arrived at Oakwood, Mrs. Ekberg told her that Luke wanted her to choose a bedroom for Bailey and decide how it should be decorated. Molly nearly dropped her briefcase. Was he so certain of her answer he'd announced to the staff that there would be a wedding? Mrs. Ekberg was matter-of-fact.

Then Molly realized that whether Bailey moved in or simply came for visits, she'd feel more comfortable if she had her own room. Molly couldn't fault Luke for that. In fact, she had to give him grudging credit for asking her advice—since no one knew better than she what Bailey liked or needed.

The next day was one of the rare ones when Warren felt up to visiting friends, and Luke invited Molly—and Bailey, of course—to stay and have dinner with him. As the three of them sat together in the dining room, Molly thought, *He's showing me what I'll be missing if I turn him down.*

And she found herself thinking, as they spent the evening like a family, that perhaps she could marry him, after all.

The following evening, when she was leaving very late, she ran into Luke on his way out of the house. She hadn't seen him wearing a tux since Megan's wedding, and to tell the truth she hadn't really seen much of anything that day—so the impact was stronger than it would otherwise have been.

Even Bailey was impressed by the tux. She stood absolutely still for an unusually long time while she looked at him, and then said, "You're pretty, Daddy," and he'd laughed and swept her up for a kiss.

But it wasn't only his faultless tailoring that made him look so good, Molly thought. There was something about his expression that spoke of exhilaration and eagerness. She couldn't help but wonder where he was going, and with whom.

The next day she found out, when Melinda the golden girl stopped by Oakwood. "I'm returning the bow tie he left at my house last night," she told Watkins. "Do tell him what a memorable evening I had, won't you?" Then she'd flashed a superior smile at Molly, who'd had the bad luck to walk through the hall just then, and departed.

Molly, a bit depressed, remembered that while Luke had said he expected their marriage would be a real one, he hadn't uttered a word about limiting himself to his wife—and she concluded that if she had any sense she'd immediately tell him no.

Shortly afterward he called her aside to tell her that his attorney had finished all the paperwork for the custody agreement, parental rights and child support—but it was up to Molly, of course, whether they signed the documents or tore them up. And—faced with the legal realities—she wavered once more.

The day after that he asked Bailey if she'd like to stay at Oakwood overnight, and she eagerly agreed, excited at the adventure. Molly's heart twisted at the thought of how easily Bailey was breaking away from her. She gritted her teeth, however, and told herself it was just as well, for this was what Bailey's future would be—moving back and forth between households. Unless, of course...

But when the time came for her mother to leave her, Bailey burst into a storm of tears, and finally Luke took her out to Molly's car. And then, to Molly's dismay, she sobbed all the way home—because she didn't have her daddy.

Molly couldn't blame the poor child for being confused when she herself hardly knew up from down. The trouble was, time was growing short. The anniversary party was tomorrow, and she still didn't know what her answer would be.

Molly hadn't known her parents had so many friends, for the guest list—like so much of the party—had been

Megan's work. The nicest part about the horde, Molly
thought, was that by the time she'd greeted each guest
the evening would be at least half over. And with the
sheer number of people—enough to make even the
Bannisters' enormous house seem crowded—avoiding
Luke would probably be no trick at all.

She crossed the atrium and ran into Megan in the dining room doorway. "I'm heartily ashamed of myself,"
she said. "All the work you put into this party, and I
haven't helped at all."

Megan shrugged. "It's what I do best—and heaven
knows I have plenty of time."

"Well, tell me what I can do right now, and go sit
down."

"Do I look that bad?"

Yes, Molly wanted to say. Megan's face looked
pinched, her eyes were shadowed, and even the rich apricot of her dress couldn't seem to reflect color to her
cheeks. "You look a little tired," she said tactfully.

A matron fluttered up and kissed Megan's cheek.
"Delightful party, darling. Where's that delicious husband of yours?"

"Rand had a business emergency. He's so sorry he
couldn't be here."

Molly had heard her utter exactly the same words,
with precisely the same inflection, at least a dozen times
since the party began. Was Rand's absence the reason
Megan seemed so drained and tired? A party this size
would be stress enough, of course, even without a missing host.

The band switched from background music to dance
numbers, the crowd fell back to leave the center of the
atrium free, and Alix and Bernie took the floor for their
anniversary waltz.

Thirty years, Molly thought. Three long decades of

living together, raising children, building a home. How had they done it?

What I really want to know is how much it mattered whether or not they loved each other. Had love been like the extra touch of spice which made a dish extraordinary, even though it tasted perfectly good without that last ingredient? Or had it been like the lubricant in an engine that kept the pieces from grating intolerably against each other, eventually to overheat and destroy the whole mechanism?

And how about a one-sided love? Would that be better or worse for a marriage than having none at all?

"I believe," Luke said behind her, "this is my dance."

With a sense of unreality, Molly stepped into his arms.

They hadn't danced together since their dutiful single turn around the floor at Megan's wedding. And he hadn't held her since that incendiary kiss in Oakwood's drive more than a week ago. She tried not to remember what that had felt like, for if she ever needed all her wits about her, it was now. But the warmth of his fingers clasping hers, the weight of his other hand at the small of her back, the brush of his cheek against her hair awakened every sensual memory from that night.

She was startled to realize, however, that in some ways this embrace was even more erotic. The ebb and flow of the music, the movement of their bodies in a rhythmic pattern sent her pulse racing. And the restraint imposed by the crowd added a piquant edge. There were so many things they couldn't do with all the world watching—and that made her want them all the more.

He whispered, "Molly, what—"

She said hastily, "Was Bailey all right? She didn't give you any trouble about staying at Oakwood, I mean? After that scene last night—"

"She was fine as soon as Watkins promised to take

her and Lucky for a walk. You're procrastinating, Molly."

Breathlessly she plunged on. "She wanted so badly to come to the party, but it's not the sort of thing for children, is it?"

"Megan's parties never are. Molly, you told me you'd answer at your parents' party. I'm waiting."

The time for analyzing was over. Molly had argued the question over and over and reached no firm conclusion. The answer would have to come from her heart.

She closed her eyes and looked deep within herself and said, "Yes."

As if on cue, the music shifted to a slower tempo, and with increased assurance Luke drew her closer. "Shall we tell everyone right now?"

He didn't sound happy about it, she thought with a trickle of uneasiness, or even particularly pleased. He sounded triumphant.

As if he'd won a battle…or maybe the whole war.

CHAPTER TEN

ANNOUNCE their engagement—when the prospective bride was already half-regretting her answer and really wanted nothing more than to climb into a damp cave and pretend to be a mushroom?

"No," Molly said hastily. "I mean… This is my parents' special night."

"Don't you think our announcement would make it even more special?"

"I think it would be very rude not to tell our families first. And what about Bailey? Surely she shouldn't be the last to know."

"I doubt she'll file a complaint with the etiquette department," Luke said dryly.

"What's the rush, anyway?" But Molly knew, of course. He wanted her to make a public commitment. The expectations of friends and family would assure she wouldn't change her mind. Luke was no fool. He understood a decision that had taken a week to form wasn't more solid than a snap decision but a whole lot more fluid.

From the corner of her eye she caught rapid movement at the far side of the atrium—people hurrying toward a patch of brilliant apricot which lay on the floor.

"It's Megan," she said. "Something's very wrong."

She pulled away from him and hurried across the room. By the time she reached the edge of the confusion, Megan was sitting up, leaning against a male guest who'd knelt beside her and trying to smile. "I felt a little faint, that's all," she said, but there was no substance to her voice. Molly could hardly hear her. "Please, go on and enjoy the party.'' She caught Molly's eye. Her gaze was a desperate plea.

Molly pushed through the crowd and sank to the floor. Her skirt formed a pool of teal-blue silk against the cold marble. ''Meg, what is it?''

''It's happening again,'' Megan whispered. ''Come with me...please?''

Another miscarriage? Oh, no... ''Try to keep me away. Will you all move back and give her some air?'' Molly looked around wildly, but she couldn't see Luke. Her mother was there, though. Alix promptly began shooing people off to the dance floor, the dining room, the terrace.

Luke appeared out of nowhere. Molly didn't want to admit the rush of relief she felt at knowing he was there beside her.

He bent over Megan. ''It's the hospital for you, my dear. I told the valet to bring my car around.''

She managed a feeble smile. ''You have something against ambulances, Hudson?''

In the Jaguar's back seat, Molly blotted perspiration from Megan's forehead. She'd thought her colorless before. Now she was pasty white.

Luke was frowning. ''How long's this been going on, Meg?''

''A couple of days. Last time it took a whole week, so I thought surely I could get through the party. And don't look at me that way, Luke. Just because I didn't want to ruin Mother and Dad's special day—''

Molly muttered, ''You should have been in bed instead of giving a party.''

''It wasn't the party that caused this. Believe me, I know the signs. And my doctor said bed rest wouldn't change a thing, so I might as well go about my normal activities.''

Much later, as Molly paced the waiting room and Luke flipped through a magazine, she said, with a trace of acid, ''I wonder if Megan's doctor knows she includes a party for three hundred in her definition of normal activities.''

Luke didn't look up from the pages of *Fortune*. ''He's probably right that it wouldn't have made a difference.''

''Shouldn't somebody try to find Rand?''

''Why? If Megan wants him, she'll ask for him.''

''That's pretty hard-hearted of you. He has a right....'' Molly's voice trailed off. *And a responsibility. If Megan knew two days ago that this was happening, and Rand went off on business anyway...*

''I see you're finally getting around to wondering why we're the ones sitting in the waiting room,'' Luke murmured. ''If we keep making visits of this frequency and duration, you know, they're going to have to put up a bronze plaque in our honor.''

''At least we're better dressed this time.''

''Speak for yourself. Given a choice between wet running shoes and a bow tie...'' He tugged the tie loose and stuffed it in his pocket. ''But as long as we're sitting here, we might as well accomplish something. There's the matter of setting a wedding date, for one thing.''

Molly's stomach tightened. ''I suppose you want to make it soon.''

''Any reason not to? A big white wedding would be in rather poor taste, so there's no real reason to delay, is there?''

I wish there was, Molly thought. But slowly, she shook her head.

Near midnight, when the worst was over, Luke left to break the news to Bernie and Alix, and Molly stayed at Megan's bedside, stroking her hair and talking softly.

''You're treating me the same way you did Bailey when she was here,'' Megan said finally.

Was the reminder of the child like salt in the wound? ''I'm sorry.''

"No—I meant it's nice to be pampered." She closed her eyes. "It's for the best, I know."

"Maybe so, though it doesn't hurt any less." Molly added carefully, "Perhaps, when you've had time to heal, you'll think about adopting. Once a baby's in your arms, it doesn't matter whether you carried him or not—"

"I know that. But Rand would never agree to giving his name to a child who wasn't of his blood, one who might have tainted genes. As if the two I've lost didn't... But of course, he's certain that's my fault. My blue-collar ancestry."

Molly was horrified at the matter-of-fact note in Megan's voice.

"I guess he thought his own blood would be rich enough to make the difference. But when I miscarried his heir... And then I couldn't seem to get pregnant again. Well, of course I was to blame. You wondered, didn't you, why I was so unhappy about what should be wonderful news?"

Molly said wryly, "I'm beginning to understand."

"I was working up my nerve to tell Rand I wanted out when I realized I was pregnant again. And I knew that if I carried the baby to term, he would consider that child his personal property—and if I divorced him, I'd lose my child just as surely as I had the first one. So I decided to keep quiet."

"You didn't even tell him?"

Megan shook her head. "If I got through the dangerous time, then of course he'd have to know. And if so, my only option would be to make the best of it. Keep a stiff upper lip and all that." She shrugged. "In a horrible way, I feel almost relieved. I'll grieve my baby, of course. But I'm not facing a life sentence any more, tied to a man who doesn't love me."

Her voice trailed off, and for a moment, Molly thought she'd drifted into sleep.

A life sentence...tied to a man who doesn't love me.

"Mother will probably never speak to me again," Megan said. "Giving up all that lovely money and my social position. It's ironic, isn't it? In the space of a couple of weeks we've changed places entirely, in her estimation. You're in the bosom of the Hudson family, and I'm an outcast."

"I don't think I'd go quite that far about either of us."

Megan didn't seem to hear. "Well, she's just going to have to lump it. As soon as Rand gets back from his business trip..."

Something about her inflection warned Molly. "It isn't a business trip?"

"Of course it isn't. He only married me because he wanted a son to carry on the dynasty and because he liked the idea of a wife who was so dependent that she could never walk out no matter how many other women he had. That part backfired, though, because if he was the one who wanted a divorce it would cost him more in a settlement. So he stayed. And I grew more miserable, until I couldn't take it any more..."

Eventually she dozed, but Molly stood for a long time beside the bed, still holding Megan's hand and listening to the chilling echo of her words.

Facing a life sentence. Tied to a man who doesn't love me. He only married me because he wanted a son.

There was an eerie familiarity to the phrases.

Luke's not Rand, Molly told herself. It wasn't fair to compare them. Nevertheless...

Megan had loved Rand once. Molly would never forget the radiance in her sister's face on her wedding day. But her love hadn't been enough to hold the marriage together. Weighed in the balance against a man who didn't love her, a man who only wanted his child, Megan's love hadn't stood a chance. Her love hadn't

changed Rand, and in the end it had been crushed to
death under the weight of her resentment and pain.

And what about Molly and her love for Luke? Would
her case be any different? Luke had been straightforward
from the beginning, as she suspected Rand hadn't. He'd
admitted he didn't love her, admitted that his main mo-
tivation was his daughter. But was honesty a substitute
for caring?

Could she afford to take the chance—with herself and
with Bailey?

Molly was lying in a lounge chair behind the house,
basking in the sunlight and catching up on her rest, when
Luke came through the sliding doors onto the deck.

He had never looked better, Molly thought. His worn
jeans hugged trim hips, and his lightweight coffee-brown
sweater made his eyes look even bigger and more inviting. As she caught his gaze he smiled at her, a slow
smile that reached straight through her and turned her
heart upside down.

But she couldn't let a smile outweigh what she knew
was right. She sat up a little straighter. "Hi. There's
some lemonade on the table."

He shook his head and pulled a chair around. "Your
mother told me Megan's here."

"She and Bailey are curled up together having a nap.
Meg didn't want to go back to that house." Molly deliberately didn't say *home*, but it was apparent Luke
knew what she meant. "And since Mother didn't disown
her, after all—"

"Megan told you everything, then?"

Molly nodded. "At least, I hope she isn't still leaving
something out. I understand why she kept quiet. The
fewer people who knew, the easier to maintain her dignity if she had to stay in the situation. But—" *But she
told you,* Molly thought. *And I want to know why.*

"It's going to be close quarters with all of you here."

"We'll make room. It probably won't be for long, anyway."

"Is that why you wanted to talk to me? We can move the wedding date up."

Molly stared at her fingernails. *Tell him. You have to tell him.*

"Remember?" Luke prompted. "You left a message for me that you wanted to talk to me about the wedding."

"I didn't put it quite that way."

"No, you were very discreet. Watkins didn't quite lose his professional demeanor, but it was plain that he was dying to know what you were talking about." He reached into his pocket. "I thought you should have this right away."

He tossed a small white velvet box into her lap. Molly picked it up, but she didn't open it. She didn't need to. The only question was what diamond cut he'd chosen and how it was set. Even the stone's size, she thought, was fairly predictable. For Luke Hudson's bride, only large would do.

If Molly hadn't already been certain of what she must do, that simple action of his would have clarified her thinking. A man in love didn't toss a diamond ring, he put it on his beloved's finger. She gave Luke some credit for not pretending a sentiment he didn't feel. But the missing tenderness was just one more piece of evidence in the chain that had brought her to this moment.

She threw the box back, and he fielded it easily. "I'm not moving the wedding up, Luke. I'm calling it off."

"You can't." He stood and dropped the box into her lap. "You gave your word."

"Well, I've changed my mind."

"No, Molly. You had more than a week to think about it. And you can't say I pestered you. I never said a thing."

No, he hadn't, she admitted. After their initial discussion, his efforts to influence her decision had been strictly nonverbal.

She followed him to the deck rail, where he stood with hands braced, and set the box carefully between his thumbs. "I'm a rat," she said. "I can't be trusted. I've led you on once. I could do it again. I've lost my mind altogether. You've had a lucky escape. Take your pick, Luke, I don't care. But let this be the end of it—so it doesn't hurt Bailey."

He picked up the velvet box and tossed it gently from one hand to the other as if he was toying with a hard-boiled egg.

"Why?"

"I told you—"

"No. I mean the reason, not the string of excuses." He didn't sound hurt or offended or resentful—only curious.

She hesitated. He'd been honest with her, she reminded herself, all the way through. Out of simple respect, she couldn't reciprocate with a lie.

But she certainly couldn't tell the truth.

She didn't look at him but at the lake, shimmering blue under the brilliant sun. "I don't think it's any of your business," she said honestly. "I've given you my decision, and it stands."

"That's what you implied last night, too—that you meant what you said." His voice was too calm, she thought, and she felt a shiver of fear. "But if your decisions are so very flexible, perhaps a little persuasion is in order."

Molly tried to move away, but his arm clamped around her and pulled her tight against him. His first kiss was demanding, almost violent—but she still couldn't keep herself entirely aloof, and with the first hint of her response his entire attitude changed. He caressed instead of attacked, asked rather than commanded. And where continued ferocity would have hardened her resolve, his gentleness seized her soul and shook it and made it even more fully his. By the time he let her go, every cell of Molly's body was trembling.

"Well, now," he drawled. "We've once more established that you're not indifferent to me."

Not that it seemed to make any real difference to him.

Shaken to the core, Molly had to take a second to compose herself before she could answer. "You're right, Luke. I'm not indifferent. Offended is more like it." She stalked across the deck and turned at the door for one last look at the man she loved. After today, he would be the father of her daughter, and nothing more.

Luke was in the midst of his mail on Wednesday morning when his secretary came in. "Excuse me, sir," she said. "But Ms. Matthews would like to speak with you. She said she'd wait."

Luke's hand clenched on the mini recorder. Molly had said she wanted to talk to him on Sunday, too—but instead she'd made her grandstand announcement and refused to discuss it. What was going on now? Yet another change of mind? "Tell her I'll be a few minutes, Wanda."

The secretary nodded and withdrew, and Luke toyed with his correspondence for a little longer, accomplishing nothing. He went to the door.

She stood the moment she saw him, and he let his gaze drift over her jade green suit. He'd thought she had the best set of legs in Minnesota, but he'd been wrong—it was more like the North American continent. With regret he stopped looking and said, "Come in, Molly."

Deliberately, he didn't indicate where she should sit. But without hesitation she chose one of the straight-backed chairs across from his desk and settled herself with a leather portfolio on her lap. "I'd like you to look over my proposals for the video portion of the history project, Luke."

Business as usual, he thought, and told himself he was neither surprised nor disappointed. Molly was obviously having no trouble separating business from personal affairs—and there was no reason he should, either.

"I actually overestimated the costs," she said, "so we can do a no-frills package and use the rest of the cash for something else, or add some extras. I've put some suggestions together to give you an idea of what I'd like to do. When you've had a chance to review this, perhaps we can discuss it." She took a neatly bound document from her portfolio and set it on his desk.

He reached for the folder and flipped through it slowly.

She didn't move, and he wondered if she was waiting for some sort of dismissal or if the video been only an excuse after all.

"There's one more thing," Molly said finally.

A curl of anticipation ran through him.

"When you hired me, Luke, we talked about recommendations to other firms. The book project is well underway and the video soon will be, so I'm starting to look for additional clients. It would be very helpful if I could use Meditronics as a reference."

Meditronics. *Not you, Luke, just your company.*

"Of course."

Molly slid to the edge of her chair.

There seemed nothing else to say, and he called himself foolish for groping for a subject, not wanting to let her go. "Megan called me last night. She said Rand finally showed up and they'd reached an agreement."

"That's one way of putting it." Molly's voice held a dry note. "It turns out the golden girl had her eyes on Rand all along. He's planning to marry Melinda."

She was watching him very closely, he thought. Was she hoping that Melinda's plans would upset him? Or hoping that they wouldn't?

"After that, it got pretty funny," Molly went on.

"Mother told Rand she didn't think he was being cheap at all, just very wise to choose a second wife with the same first initial so he didn't have to change the monograms on the towels." She stood. "But I shouldn't take up your time with gossip. You'll let me know, won't you, when you've had a chance to review my suggestions?"

She crossed the office so quickly that there was no point in going after her to hold the door. Instead, he stood by his desk and watched the enticing sway of that slim skirt. "Molly—"

She turned, eyebrows raised.

He hadn't meant to call her name. He wasn't certain why he'd done so, and he was embarrassingly tongue-tied.

"Is there something else, Luke?"

"No. I mean... If you don't have plans this evening, I'd like to take Bailey home with me."

"Of course. Do you want to pick her up from day care?"

He nodded, and she was gone with a friendly little wave.

She was as casual, he thought, as if there had never been anything between them. No evening of passion years ago. No sultry, seductive kisses. No less-than-a-day-long engagement.

Why had she changed her mind? It was none of his business, she'd said. An absolutely foolish statement, of course. If her reasons for rejecting him weren't his business, what in hell was?

What was it she hadn't been able to stomach?

Of course, it was a terrible sacrifice he'd asked her to make, he thought sardonically. To live at Oakwood with its elegance and its devoted staff. To work only if she wanted to, not because she had to put food in her daughter's mouth. To have every day with her child. To wear his ring...

He took the velvet box from his desk drawer and watched the stones flash fire as he turned the ring.

There was certainly nothing wrong with the ring. She hadn't even bothered to look at it.

To marry me. That, of course, was the crux of it.

He put the ring on the desk blotter and rubbed his temples.

And he wondered if someday he'd be able to forget the taste of her.

Bailey had crept into bed with Molly in the middle of the night, and still sound asleep, she was taking up far more than her fair share of space. *What a way to start Mother's Day,* Molly thought as she yawned and got up.

Her father was in the kitchen, stirring his special pancakes. "Be a good girl and take your mother coffee, will you?" he asked.

Molly got a bone china mug from the cabinet and carried the steaming coffee down the hall to the master bedroom where Alix was sitting up in bed, propped with pillows, reading *Vogue.*

"Your coffee, madam," Molly said. "Happy Mother's Day."

Alix laid the magazine aside. "I suppose Bernie's being silly about pancakes?"

"Well, please don't stop him. I love his pancakes." Molly sat on the edge of the bed. "Mother, I just wanted to tell you I'm sorry. I know I've been a huge disappointment." *And now that I'm not going to marry Luke, I'm no doubt shaming you all over again.*

Alix sipped her coffee and stared across the room until Molly wondered if she was going to ignore the apology altogether.

"I wasn't disappointed with you," Alix said slowly, "but with myself. You frightened me—your depth, your independence, your intelligence…"

"My stubbornness?"

Alix smiled. "Maybe that, too. Megan was so easy as a teenager, so open. She had to wait till now to turn into a mystery. No doubt the struggle she's having is because of the way I raised her—to be too sensitive to what others would think. But you—even when you faced the worst time of your life, you wouldn't let me in. I know I didn't go about it very well—"

"You did what you thought was best, Mom."

Alix shook her head. "No. I'm sorry, Molly, for the stories I told. I even managed to convince myself that I honestly intended them for your protection, when all the time... Now I don't know if I should correct all my lies, or if that would only make things worse for you."

"Leave it alone, Mom." Molly leaned over to give Alix a hug, and her mother held her tightly for a very long time.

Bailey came in, dragging a stuffed lion by the tail, and climbed into Alix's lap. "Gramma, I drew you a picture for Mother's Day."

"Did you, darling? I'll frame it." Alix nestled her close. "I am so very proud of you, Molly—and of my granddaughter."

Bailey snuggled into Alix's arms and yawned.

At least, Molly thought, something was turning out right.

After breakfast Molly took Bailey for a drive and pulled her car off the road near the child's favorite beach. *You're asking for heartache,* she told herself. Coming here, where she'd told Bailey about her father, was guaranteed to be painful—but if she lived in Duluth she couldn't stay away from this stretch of shoreline forever. And it was hardly the lake's fault.

"Daddy lets me bring Lucky," Bailey pointed out. But she took off down the beach, tromping along the edge of the water and now and then sending up a giant splash when a bigger-than-usual wave surprised her.

Molly sat on the driftwood log where she'd broken the news and started drawing patterns in the pebbly beach. She didn't know how long she'd been sitting there when a red-gold streak flashed past her and toward the water, barking wildly. She jumped up, panicked, helpless to get between Bailey and the dog that threatened her—until she realized it was Lucky.

Which meant, of course, that Luke was very near. She closed her eyes to try to gather strength.

His jeans and running shoes contrasted oddly with the gold foil wrapping and enormous ribbons on the box he carried under one arm. "Hi," he said. "Your dad told me you'd come up this way, and then I saw the car." He held out the box. "Happy Mother's Day."

She didn't want to open it. But he meant well, and she could hardly fling his gift back in his face. So she sat on the driftwood log once more and slowly began to pull the tape loose.

Luke sat beside her, a careful foot away. He leaned forward to scoop up a handful of pebbles and let them sift slowly through his fingers.

As soon as she saw the box, Molly's stomach churned in protest. It wasn't only unfair and manipulative, she thought, it was absolutely tasteless of him to buy her a gift at Milady Lingerie. Even if he'd chosen something innocuous, just the suggestive simplicity of the box sent a message that she didn't want to hear.

The gift inside was far from innocent. She folded back the gold tissue paper to reveal a satin and lace teddy in a soft shade of emerald green—exactly the color to make her skin glow and her eyes shine. It was even, she noted, precisely the right size.

She stared at it for a moment and gritted her teeth against the pain. As if she was shallow enough to let a sexy bit of lingerie affect her judgment! Didn't he even begin to understand that physical attraction wasn't enough, that feelings were overwhelmingly important?

"This isn't funny, Luke." She folded the tissue in place, her hands trembling. "It's inappropriate and insulting."

As soon as I can keep my voice from shaking, she thought, *I'll call for Bailey, and we'll leave. Only a moment more...*

"I'm sorry," he said.

She didn't look at him, but she nodded, in acceptance though not agreement. He'd never truly understand, she knew. So she might as well not break her heart over it—or waste her time trying to explain.

"Not for the lingerie," he said. "For...a long time ago."

Molly sat very still.

"My mother," Luke said slowly. "I adored her, you know. Two weeks before she died, I came home for her birthday and she was—appeared to be—in perfect health. Then in a moment, she collapsed. They told us she was dying. And I couldn't do anything to save her. My time in med school had been worse than useless—I only knew enough to understand how bad it was."

Molly put out a hand to him, but he seemed too enclosed in his mind to see it.

"That night in the treehouse was the worst as I struggled to accept that I was losing her. Then suddenly you were there, only trying to help.... Molly, I felt so guilty for taking advantage of you."

"You didn't. I threw myself at you." Bitterness crept into her voice. "That was painfully clear when you couldn't bring yourself to go through with it, to actually make love to me...."

"That was never the problem. What terrified me was how much I wanted you—when I knew you had no idea what you were doing."

A cool breeze stirred Molly's hair and made the gold foil paper rustle. "I was already embarrassed and ashamed, and when you took me aside a few days later and made it clear what you thought of me..." She bit her lip. "When I found out the impossible had happened and I was going to have your child..."

"I understand why you didn't tell me."

"Oh, you've finally figured it out! What was I supposed to do, Luke? You'd made it absolutely plain that you didn't want to see me ever again, that there was nothing about me you found attractive—"

"There were lots of things even then. Now..." He drew a deep breath. "Your dignity in the face of uncertainty and trouble. Bailey—and the fact that you brought her into the world with the situation you were in. There were easier ways."

Molly shook her head. "Not for me."

"Then there's my father—I wouldn't be surprised if he proposes to you yet when he discovers that you've turned me down. The staff would lie on the floor and let you clean your shoes on them. In fact, the only living creature at Oakwood who isn't totally in love with you—"

Is the one I care most about, she thought sadly.

"Is the dog, and that's only because you scold her adored playmate once in a while."

Every muscle in Molly's body tightened like an overwound spring. Did he realize what he'd said? And if so, did he—could he—actually mean it?

"And then there's me." Luke cleared his throat. "I said all those years ago that you were too young to know what love was. And I still think I was right. But I didn't recognize love, either. When you refused me last week, I was furious. To throw aside an opportunity like the one I'd offered you..."

Molly wanted to say, *And what an opportunity! All the material things and nothing that really mattered.*

"I tried to be logical, to figure it out. Obviously, it wasn't Oakwood that you disliked. And though you weren't greedy when it came to money, I didn't think you hated the stuff enough to refuse me on the grounds that I had too much of it. And it was apparent there was very little you wouldn't do for Bailey. So that left marriage itself—or rather, marriage to me—that you found so distasteful.''

She wanted to say, *Not if it could be a real marriage.* But she had lost control of her voice.

"And that was when I realized I wasn't angry, after all. I was hurt, and terribly sad that you didn't care about me. That even for Bailey's sake you couldn't face sharing a life with me. And yet when you kissed me..."

"There's more to being married than sharing a bed, Luke."

"Yeah." He picked up the lingerie box. "This was really a bad idea, wasn't it?"

"I don't know," Molly said carefully. "It depends on why you did it."

"To tell you that the reason I want you isn't that you're Bailey's mother. But I miscalculated, didn't I? Because I don't just want you to be my wife in the bedroom, either, but everywhere. All the time. Forever. I love you, Molly."

Her hands were squeezed so tightly together that her knuckles were white.

"Yes, I want Bailey," he said. "I don't want to be a part-time father to my little girl. That's fact, and there's no sense dodging it. But it wasn't Bailey I thought of last Sunday when you so much as told me to go jump off the aerial lift bridge. I thought of myself—and how empty my life was going to be. Not because I wouldn't have Bailey...but because I wouldn't have you." He fitted the top on the lingerie box. "I'm sorry, Molly. For everything."

He was ten feet away before she found her voice. "What are you going to do with my Mother's Day gift, Luke?"

He didn't look back. "Probably start by ripping it

apart with my bare hands. Then I might— Do you mean
you want it?''

"I didn't turn you down because I found you distasteful, Luke. I did it because I knew it would tear me apart
to live with a man who didn't love me when I loved you
so much I drove myself crazy trying to find any reason
to believe we could make it work.''

The box went spinning to the ground. Luke seized
Molly's hands and pulled her into his arms, and she discovered that kisses were even better when there were no
secrets left between them.

"You were so casual." Luke sounded a little breathless. Molly wasn't surprised. "So cool—in the office.
As if you'd forgotten…everything.''

Molly shrugged. "Acting that way wasn't the most
fun I've ever had, that's sure. But we were going to have
to deal with each other for years to come—till Bailey
grew up, at least. And I knew if I slipped and let you
see what I was going through, and if you felt sorry for
me—''

"I wouldn't have had time to feel sorry for you, I was
too busy staring at a ring you wouldn't wear and feeling
sorry for myself.'' He pulled the velvet box from his
pocket. "Want it?''

The box looked dingy and a bit the worse for wear,
Molly thought, as if he'd been carrying it for days.
"Yes.'' She reached for the box, but Luke held it out
of her reach while he extracted the ring and used one
hand to shield it from view till he'd slipped it into place
on her finger.

Molly held out her hand. She'd never seen an emerald
so brilliant, so richly colored, so perfect.

"It's the color of your eyes," he said. "Only I was
too deluded when I bought it to know why that was so
important.'' She started to cry, and he kissed her tears
away. After a while, he said, "Now are we going to set
a wedding date, or shall I call Rand for his preferred list

of love nests and carry you off to one of them and make love to you so often you can't remember your name, much less your objections?''

"I'll bet your choice would be better than his."

"Is that a challenge, Ms. Matthews? I'll see what I can do."

"You weren't surprised about Melinda, were you?"

"Of course not. I'd thought for a long time that she and Rand were just a little too formal with each other to be real."

"But you were dating her anyway?" Molly sounded doubtful.

"Only in the spirit of collecting information for Megan. It wasn't difficult, because Melinda always had an eye out for an extra man, and she must have thought I'd make especially good cover since I was Megan's friend."

"And that's why you and Megan were meeting in out-of-the-way ice cream shops? You were reporting?"

"I wasn't going to go into detail where her maid might be able to hear. But how'd you know that?"

"Bailey spotted you." Molly shook her head. "Next time you try to go undercover, Luke, you might drive something besides a Jaguar."

"I'll keep it in mind. The final confirmation was that Rand made the reservations for their little weekend in Melinda's name and sent the tickets to her with a very juicy note."

"And I suppose she told you all about it?"

"I snooped," Luke said cheerfully. "But I didn't have to work very hard at it. She'd left the package right on her desk, and I had plenty of time to browse while I was waiting for her to finish dressing for the opera."

The night, Molly thought, that he'd left Oakwood looking eager and full of anticipation—not because he was going to see Melinda, but because he was hoping to catch her red-handed. "Just don't get in the habit of leaving your bow ties in other women's houses."

"And you think she took it off me in a passionate interlude? Sorry to disappoint you, darling, but I never wear those things any longer than necessary."

She remembered him tugging his tie off in the hospital while they were waiting out Megan's miscarriage and stuffing it in his pocket.

"I must have dropped it. I'm only surprised she didn't deliver it to Megan as a smoke screen."

"She probably figured the message would get passed along," Molly said dryly. "There is one more thing, Luke. About that teddy—how'd you know what size to buy?"

"Would you believe I walked into the shop and told the clerk that you were just about this shape—" He demonstrated.

"No."

"I didn't think so. The truth, unfortunately, is much less romantic. You were still in their computer from the last time you bought something in the Chicago store. So not only did I know what size to buy, but exactly the kind of thing you like—and if you think *that* didn't start affecting my dreams…"

He bent once more to kiss her and paused to stroke her cheek. "That bruise on your jaw. You never did tell me how you got it."

"I told you it was nothing. Bailey was demonstrating her new gymnastic tricks for me, but somehow she stretched out instead of tucking in, and she kicked me. Almost knocked me down."

"Why didn't you tell me that in the beginning?"

"Because the first time you asked, you didn't even know about her, and the last thing I wanted to do was explain."

He considered and nodded. "And your broken leg? Bailey said you fell down the stairs."

Molly frowned. "And you thought I'd been pushed? No, I slipped on a patch of ice at the top of a flight of concrete steps."

"I'm glad."

"That I broke my leg?"

"That you weren't battered. Every time I thought about that bruise, I felt guilty, because if my clumsiness had made you turn to a man like that…"

She turned her head away so he couldn't see her face and admitted, "Luke, I know this sounds crazy. My daughter's almost four. But that time—with you—was the only…" She paused. "I've never…"

He was silent and still for so long that she began to regret her confession. "Surely there were other men."

"I dated. But there was nobody like you."

"At times," Luke said dryly, "that must have seemed a blessing. My darling… I'll make it up to you. All of it—I swear."

He kissed her again, long and deeply, and Molly came back to earth only when a little hand tugged firmly at her sweater. "Mommy," Bailey said indignantly. "Daddy. I want a hug, too!"

So they picked up their daughter and held her between them, and Bailey put an arm around each neck and drew them closer yet.

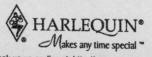

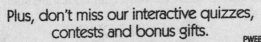

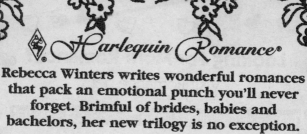

Harlequin Romance®

Rebecca Winters writes wonderful romances that pack an emotional punch you'll never forget. Brimful of brides, babies and bachelors, her new trilogy is no exception.

Meet Annabelle, Gerard and Diana. Annabelle and Gerard are private investigators, Diana, their hardworking assistant. Each of them is about to face a rather different assignment—falling in love!

LOVE
undercover

Their mission was marriage!

Books in this series are:

**March 1999 #3545
UNDERCOVER FIANCÉE**

**April 1999 #3549
UNDERCOVER BACHELOR**

**MAY 1999 #3553
UNDERCOVER BABY**

Available wherever Harlequin books are sold.

HARLEQUIN®
Makes any time special ™

Look us up on-line at: http://www.romance.net

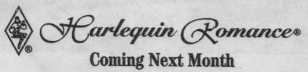

Harlequin Romance®
Coming Next Month

#3555 THE BOSS AND THE PLAIN JAYNE BRIDE
Heather MacAllister

Jayne Nelson feels her life lacks pizzazz. She's just spent her twenty-eighth birthday working overtime for her accounting firm. Then Garrett Charles walks into her life. Talk about pizzazz! Though Jayne realizes he's out of her league, that doesn't stop her daydreams becoming X-rated! But Jayne wants more than dreams…

#3556 TO CLAIM A WIFE Susan Fox

Caitlin Bodine is the black sheep of her family—and Reno Duvall certainly blames her for his brother's death. For five years, he's cut her out of his life. Now he's forced to share his ranch with this beautiful, heartless woman. He doesn't like it one bit, and neither does Caitlin! Only, living together, they discover how they've misjudged each other. Reno wasn't looking for a wife, but he becomes determined to claim Caitlin for his own…

Rebel Brides: *Two rebellious cousins—and the men who tame them!*

Meet Caitlin and Maddie: two beautiful, spirited cousins seeking to overcome family secrets and betrayal. As they come to terms with past tragedy, their proud, rebellious hearts are tamed by two powerful ranchers who won't take no for an answer!

Look out in July for **To Tame a Bride.**

#3557 THE PARENT TRAP Ruth Jean Dale

Matt Reynolds finds Laura Gilliam infuriating—and the feeling is more than mutual. Unfortunately, their kids have decided that they'd make a perfect match! But though Matt realizes that his little girl needs a mother and Laura that her little boy needs a dad, they're determined not to fall into the parent trap! But is it too late?

#3558 FALLING FOR JACK Trisha David

Jack Morgan has been left to bring up his small daughter Maddy single-handedly. It wasn't easy. Then Bryony Lester fell into their lives. Maddy warmed to her instantly—how could Jack resist a woman who could make Maddy smile?

Daddy Boom: *Who says babies and bachelors don't mix?*